Emily of New Moon

Don't miss L. M. Montgomery's *Anne of Green Gables*,
adapted by Shelley Tanaka.

And for the complete story of Emily, look for these
books in your bookstore or library:

Emily of New Moon

Emily Climbs

Emily's Quest

Emily of New Moon

by
L. M. Montgomery

Adapted by Priscilla Galloway

DELACORTE PRESS

Published by
Delacorte Press
Bantam Doubleday Dell Publishing Group, Inc.
1540 Broadway
New York, New York 10036

Library of Congress Cataloging-in-Publication Data

Galloway, Priscilla.
    Emily of New Moon / adapted by Priscilla Galloway.
       p.   cm.
    Summary: When Emily's father dies, leaving her an orphan, she is
sent to live with a stern aunt in Prince Edward Island, where her
resourcefulness and love of writing help her adjust to a new way of
life.
    ISBN 0-385-32506-1
    [1. Orphans—Fiction.   2. Aunts—Fiction.   3. Prince Edward
Island—Fiction.   4. Authorship—Fiction.]   I. Montgomery, L. M.
(Lucy Maud), 1874–1942. Emily of New Moon.   II. Title.
PZ7.G1385Em   1997
[Fic]—dc21   97-4255
                                                   CIP
                                                   AC

The text of this book is set in 13-point Perpetua.
Book design by Patrice Sheridan
Manufactured in the United States of America

March 1998

10 9 8 7 6 5 4 3 2 1

Contents

Chapter 1

Emily and Her Father

"I wouldn't stay another night in that lonely house," said Ellen Greene, "if I wasn't so sorry for the child."

"The child," however, was never lonely. Emily Byrd Starr had all the company she wanted: Father, and Mike, and Saucy Sal, not to mention the Wind Woman and her special trees. And there was "the flash," when Emily felt all was right in her world. She never knew when the flash might come.

Emily had slipped away in the chilly May twilight for a walk. She remembered that walk all her life, partly because the flash came for the first time in weeks, but mostly because of what happened after she came back.

Father had lain quietly all day on the couch. He didn't even look at the two big spruce trees in the front yard. Emily had named them Adam-and-Eve because they stood so stiffly, one on each side of a squat little apple tree, looking just like the picture of Adam and Eve and the tree of knowledge in one of Ellen Greene's books.

Emily wished she had someone to talk to, but she never bothered Father when his cough was bad. Ellen Greene had hardly said a word since the doctor's visit last night, but Ellen was never good company. Emily had spent the afternoon curled up in the ragged old wing chair, reading her favorite book.

Douglas Starr didn't want any supper. "You go and eat," he told Emily. "I'll lie here and rest. Afterwards, we'll have a real talk, Elfkin."

He smiled his old, beautiful, loving smile, and Emily ate her supper happily, although the bread was soggy and her egg was almost raw. For once, Ellen allowed her to have her cats beside her, and only grunted when Emily fed them bits of bread. Mike was her favorite, soft and fat and fluffy, with huge owl-like eyes. Saucy Sal was a fighter and too thin to cuddle. Emily worried because Saucy Sal didn't have kittens, but she loved them both.

By the time supper was over, her father had fallen asleep. Emily was glad, because he had not slept much for two nights. She was also sorry, because they would not have their special talk. But she could go for a walk, for the first time in months. She had had to stay inside all winter because of the snow, and all through April because of the wind and rain.

"Put on your hood, and scoot back if it starts to rain," warned Ellen. "You can't fool with a cold the way some kids can."

"Why not?" asked Emily. "It's not fair." But Ellen only grunted. Emily ran upstairs to get her old blue hood. She pulled it over her long, heavy braid of jet-black hair, and smiled at herself in the mirror. The smile began at the corners of her lips and spread over her face. It was her mother's smile, and her father loved it dearly. In every other way Emily looked like the Starrs, her father's family—in her large, purplish gray eyes with their long lashes and black brows, in her high, white forehead, oval face and sensitive mouth, and in her little pointed elf-ears.

"I'm going for a walk with the Wind Woman," said Emily, smiling at her reflection. "She's an old, old friend of mine, though not quite as old as we are, little Emily-in-the-glass. I wish you could come too." Emily blew a kiss to Emily-in-the-mirror and ran downstairs.

The Wind Woman was waiting outside, teasing

the Rooster Pine behind the house—it did look like a rooster, with an enormous bunchy tail and a huge, ridiculous head thrown back to crow.

Emily felt like a prisoner let out of jail as she skimmed over the bare field toward little clumps of spruces. She was small and pale, shivering in her thin jacket. Nobody looking at her would have been envious, yet a queen might have traded her crown for Emily's visions. The mossy, half-dead spruce tree was a marble column in a magic palace. The hills were walls around an enchanted city. Elves of white clover and the little green folk of the grass kept her company. Emily played hide-and-seek with the Wind Woman around the trees. Then suddenly the wind was gone, and the evening was bathed in silence. Clouds parted to show a pale, pinky green lake of sky and a sliver of new moon.

Emily stood and looked up. The sky was so beautiful it hurt. Soon she would go home and describe the scene in her special yellow book; later, she would read what she had written to Father.

Then came "the flash." It was as if a wind fluttered the curtain between some unseen, wondrous world and herself, and she caught a glimpse of it, or heard a note of heavenly music. The flash came rarely and went quickly, always leaving her breathless with joy. It never came twice because of the same thing. Tonight the dark branches against the far-off sky had brought it. Other times it had come with a wild note of wind in the night, with a gray bird lighting on her windowsill in a storm, or with a nighttime glimpse of the kitchen fire.

Emily scuttled back home. Ellen Greene was waiting on the doorstep. Emily was so full of happiness that she loved everything right then. She flung her arms around Ellen and hugged her. Ellen looked down gloomily into the joyous little face and said, "Do you know your pa has only a week or two more to live?"

Emily was as stunned as if Ellen had slapped her. The color faded from her face, and her pupils grew large, turning her eyes into pools of blackness. Even Ellen Greene felt uncomfortable.

"It's high time you was told," she said. "I've been at your pa for months. 'It's your duty to prepare her,' says I. But he's never said a word, and when the doctor told me last night the end might come any time now, I made up my mind to tell you myself. Goodness gracious, child, don't look like that! You ma's people hate your pa like p'ison, but they'll look after you. The Murray pride will see to that! They'll give you a good home, better'n here.

"As for your pa, you ought to be thankful to see him at rest. He's been dying by inches for the last five years. Folks say his heart broke when your ma died so sudden-like. That's why I want you to know what's coming, so you won't be all upset when it happens. For mercy's sake, Emily Byrd Starr, don't stare like that! You give me the creeps! And don't go pestering your pa about what I've told you. Come in, and I'll give you a cookie 'fore you go to bed.''

Ellen stepped down as if to take Emily's hand. With a sharp, bitter little cry, Emily darted through the door and fled up the dark staircase.

Ellen waddled back to her kitchen. "Anyhow, I've done *my* duty,'' she told herself. "She'll brace up in a day or two. She's got spunk, and a good thing too, from what I hear of the Murrays. I wish I dared send them word that he's dying, but I don't dast go that far. Here, you Sal-thing, git outside. Where's Mike?"

Mike was upstairs, clutched in Emily's arms. "If I was God I wouldn't let things like this happen," Emily said. She felt very wicked, finding fault with God. But she didn't care. Maybe God would strike her dead and she and Father could go on being together. But nothing happened, except that Mike got tired of being squeezed so tight and squirmed away.

When her Sunday school teacher had moved, when she had been hungry at night, or when Ellen had told her she must be crazy to talk about Wind Women and flashes, Emily had written in her yellow book, and afterward these things hadn't hurt her anymore. But this was too terrible to write about. Father was going to die in a week or two. "The flash will never come again," Emily told herself.

Father coughed in the room below. Quickly Emily undressed and crept into bed. When he came into the room, she was lying there cold and still. How slowly he walked. Why had she never noticed? Douglas Starr sat down on the chair beside her. Oh, how she loved him! There was no other father like him in all the world.

"Winkums, are you asleep?"

"No," whispered Emily.

Douglas Starr took her hand and held it tight. "I want to tell you something," he said.

"Oh, Father, I know it," burst out Emily. "Ellen told me."

"How dare she!" Douglas Starr exclaimed.

"It isn't true, is it?" whispered Emily.

"Dear Emilykin, it is quite true," he said. "I meant to tell you myself tonight. Ellen has the brain of a hen and the sensibility of a cow."

Emily choked. "Father, I can't bear it."

"Yes, you can. You will. Darling, do you remember your mother?"

"A little, like lovely dreams."

"You were only four when she died. Emily, your mother was the sweetest woman. She was tall and fair and blue-eyed, a little like your aunt Laura, but prettier. She was one of the Murrays from Blair Water. They've lived up there on New Moon Farm since the first Murray came from England in 1790."

"It's a nice name," whispered Emily.

"They're proud, the Murrays. They do have things to be proud of, but they carry it too far. Only three of them live at New Moon Farm now, your aunts Elizabeth and Laura, and their cousin Jimmy. They never married—couldn't find anyone good enough for a Murray, folks used to say. You've got two other uncles and an aunt who don't live at the farm. Then there's your grandfather's sister, your great-aunt Nancy. She lives at Priest Pond."

"Priest Pond, that's an interesting name," said Emily. Her father kissed her black head. For a moment she almost forgot her fears.

"Elizabeth and Laura and the other three were your grandfather's first family. When he was sixty, he married again, and your mother, Juliet, was born. She was twenty years younger than any of the others, and they treated her like a princess. When she wanted to marry me, a poor young journalist, there was a family earthquake. The Murray pride couldn't put up with it at all. Your mother ran away to marry me, Emily, and the New Moon people never spoke to her or wrote to her again. Can you believe she was never sorry?''

''Of course she was never sorry. She had you.''

''We were so happy, Emilykin. You were the child of that happiness.''

''I wish people could remember from the very moment they're born,'' said Emily. ''It would be so interesting.''

Her father laughed a little. ''It can't be easy getting used to living, any more than getting used to stopping it,'' he said. ''Do you remember when your mother died?''

''I remember the funeral, Father. Mother was lying in a long, black box. You were crying, and I wondered why she wouldn't open her eyes.''

''The Murrays all came to her funeral. They came when she was dead. They would have come when she was ill if they had known, I will say that much for them. And they behaved very well. They offered to take you and bring you up, but I refused. Was I right, Emily?''

"Yes, yes," whispered Emily, hugging him hard.

"I have no money to leave you, dearest, but your mother's people will take care of you. They are too proud to do anything else. I'm sure they'll love you. Maybe I should have sent for them, but they did say some very bitter things when I married your mother, and I have some pride as well. Should I send for them now, Emily?''

"No," said Emily fiercely.

"We'll stay together to the end, then, Emily-child. I don't want you to be afraid of *anything*. The universe is full of love. Death isn't terrible. In death you open and shut a door. I'll find your mother on the other side of that door, and we'll wait for you.''

"I wish you could take me now," whispered Emily.

"Life has many wonders for you, Emily. You can't see it now, but you'll feel differently later, and you'll remember what I've said.''

Father's arms tightened around her, and Emily found her fear slipping away and the pain going out of her heart. Father would be on the other side of a door—no, a curtain. Emily liked that idea better, a curtain that wavered between this world and that other world, the world of love and beauty she had glimpsed through the flash.

Chapter 2

*R*elatives

Douglas Starr lived for two more weeks. They were beautiful weeks, beautiful and not sad. And one night he went past the curtain, so quietly that Emily did not know he was gone until she felt the strange *stillness* of the room, where there was no breathing but her own.

Emily cried all night, but when morning came her tears were done. She was quiet and pale.

"Mrs. Hubbard's fixing a black dress for you. It'll be ready by suppertime," Ellen said. "Your ma's people sent a telegram, and they'll be here tonight. Have you been in to see the body?"

"Don't call him *that*." Emily winced.

"Why not? He makes a better-looking corpse than I thought he would. He was always a pretty man, though too thin."

"Ellen Greene," said Emily suddenly, "if you say any more of those things about Father, I will put the black curse on you."

Ellen Greene stared. "That's no way to talk to me, after all I've done for you. You'd better not let the Murrays hear you talking like that. The black curse indeed!"

Emily's eyes smarted. She did feel lonely now, with Father gone, but she was not sorry for what she had said and would not pretend she was.

"Come and help me wash the dishes," ordered Ellen. "If your aunt Ruth takes you, she'll soon cure you of black curses and such."

"Is Aunt Ruth going to take me?"

"She ought to. She's a widow with no chick or child, and well-to-do."

"I don't think I want Aunt Ruth to take me," Emily decided.

"It won't be your choice! You'd better be thankful for a home. You're not important."

"I am important to myself," cried Emily proudly.

"It'll be some chore to bring *you* up," muttered Ellen. "I think your aunt Ruth is the one to do it. She's the neatest housekeeper on Prince Edward Island. She'd learn you some sense."

"I don't want to learn sense," cried Emily. "I—I want somebody to love me."

"You're a queer child," said Ellen. "It comes of not mixing with other children. I was after your father to send you to school, but he wouldn't listen to me, of course. In a way it would be good if your uncle Oliver took you. He has a big family, but he isn't well off, so I don't suppose he will. Your uncle Wallace might, he's only got a grown-up daughter. But his wife isn't strong."

"I wish Aunt Laura would take me," said Emily. Father had said Aunt Laura was like her mother.

"Aunt Laura! She won't have no say in it. Elizabeth's boss at New Moon. Jimmy Murray runs the farm, but he ain't quite all there, I'm told—"

"What part of him isn't there?" asked Emily curiously.

"Laws, it's something about his mind, some accident when he was a child. Elizabeth was mixed up in it somehow. But the New Moon people are set in their ways. I don't reckon they'll want to be bothered with you. You take my advice and try to please your aunt Ruth. There, that's all the dishes. You better go upstairs and be out of the way."

Emily went upstairs and curled up on her bed. She wanted to cry, but she did not want the Murrays, who had hated her father, to see her crying. "There isn't anybody in the world who loves me now," she said.

When the far-off whistle of the afternoon train blew, Emily's heart began to beat hard. Soon there was the sound of wheels below, and loud, decided voices. Ellen came puffing up the stairs with the dress, a flimsy thing of cheap black cotton, and Emily quickly slipped it on.

"All the Murrays are here," said Ellen. "This dress was done just in time. I wouldn't want the Murrays to see you not in black. They can't say I haven't done my duty by you. Come along."

Emily walked rigidly downstairs and into the parlor. Eight people stared at her. She looked pale and plain in the black dress, and her eyes were large and hollow with crying. She was dreadfully afraid, but determined not to let the Murrays see it. She held her head up high.

"This is your uncle Wallace," said Ellen.

Emily put out her hand. Uncle Wallace was grim and ugly, with bristly eyebrows and a stern mouth.

"How do you do, Emily?" he said, and bent forward coldly to kiss her cheek.

A wave of rage swept over Emily. How dared he kiss her, this man who had hated her father and disowned her mother? She snatched her handkerchief from her pocket and wiped her cheek.

"Well—*well!*" exclaimed a voice from the other side of the room.

Ellen sighed and pushed Emily on. "Your aunt Eva," she said. Aunt Eva shook hands silently.

"Your uncle Oliver," announced Ellen.

Uncle Oliver was fat and rosy. "I'll give you a quarter for a kiss," he said, chuckling.

Emily didn't know he was teasing her. "I don't *sell* my kisses," she said haughtily. Uncle Oliver laughed.

Aunt Addie was next. She was as fat and jolly-looking as her husband, and she gave Emily's hand a gentle squeeze. "How are you, dear?" she said.

The "dear" touched Emily, but she froze again at once. Next was Aunt Ruth. Emily knew it was Aunt Ruth before Ellen said so, and she knew it was Aunt Ruth who had "well—welled" and sniffed. She knew the cold, gray eyes; the dull, brown hair; the thin, pinched, unforgiving mouth. Aunt Ruth held out the tips of her fingers, but Emily did not take them.

"Shake hands," hissed Ellen.

"She does not want to shake hands with me," said Emily, "and I am not going to do it."

"You are a rude child," said Aunt Ruth. "Just as I expected."

Emily felt guilty. Had she let Father down? Perhaps she should have shaken hands with Aunt Ruth. But Ellen had jerked her on.

"Your cousin James Murray," she said.

"Cousin Jimmy." He smiled. Emily looked steadily at him and liked him at once. He had a rosy, elfish face with a forked gray beard; his hair was an un-Murray-like mop of brown curls, and his big brown eyes were kind as a child's. He gave Emily a hearty handshake. "Hello, kitten," he said.

Emily started to smile, but Ellen had jerked her on again, to Aunt Laura, who had delicate features and heavy coils of pale, fair hair pinned closely round her head.

"Juliet's smile," she said, and again Aunt Ruth sniffed. "You poor, dear child," she said, and put her arms around Emily.

Emily returned the hug. Now she almost let the Murrays see her cry, but Ellen pushed her on. "And this is your aunt Elizabeth."

Aunt Elizabeth wore a stiff, rich black satin dress. She was tall and thin, with a crown of iron-gray hair under her black lace cap. But her eyes were as cold as Aunt Ruth's. Emily would have liked to please

Aunt Elizabeth, who was "boss" at New Moon, but she felt she could not do it. Aunt Elizabeth shook hands and said nothing. Aunt Elizabeth did not know what to say. She did not want Emily to snub her as she had Wallace and Ruth.

"Go sit on the sofa," ordered Ellen, retreating to the kitchen.

Emily sat. She folded her hands politely and crossed her ankles. She longed to be somewhere else. In the back of her mind, however, she was already writing about this meeting in her old yellow book. She could describe them all. Aunt Ruth's eyes, for instance, were "stone-gray," as hard and cold as rock. Aunt Laura's eyes? "Wells of blue," the very thing! And then the flash came!

It was the first time after that horrible night when Ellen had met her on the doorstep. Emily had been sure it would never come again, and now it *had* come! Emily lifted her head. Yes, she would write about them all, from sweet Aunt Laura to grim Uncle Wallace and nasty Aunt Ruth.

"She's a delicate-looking child," said Aunt Eva suddenly.

"She's not a Murray," said Aunt Elizabeth disapprovingly.

"She's not a Starr either," said Uncle Oliver.

"More like the Byrds, I'd say; she's got her grandmother's hair and eyes."

"She's got her father's forehead," said Aunt Eva, also disapprovingly.

"You're talking about me as if I wasn't here," Emily protested.

The Murrays stared at her. "When I was a girl," said Aunt Ruth, "I never spoke until I was spoken to."

"If nobody spoke until they were spoken to, nobody would ever say anything at all," argued Emily.

"I never answered back," Aunt Ruth went on grimly. "In my day little girls were polite and respectful to their elders."

"I don't think you had much fun," said Emily, and bit her lip. She had not meant to say it out loud.

Aunt Ruth looked as if she wanted to box Emily's ears. "Fun!" she echoed. "I did not think of having fun when I was a little girl."

Luckily, Ellen Greene came in just then. "Supper's ready," she said. "You'll have to wait," she told Emily. "There's no room for you at the table."

"Thank goodness," Emily told herself. She knew she could not eat a bite in front of the Murrays. Now that she was alone, her pride left her. Tears prickled her eyes. She opened the other door and went into

the little room where her father's coffin lay. She
curled up on the floor and put her cheek against the
polished wood. They found her there asleep after
supper.

Aunt Laura lifted her. "I'll take the child up to
bed," she told them. "She's worn right out."

Emily opened sleepy eyes. "Can I have Mike?"
she asked.

"Who is Mike?"

"My cat."

"A cat in your bedroom!" exclaimed Aunt Elizabeth. "Certainly not. It's most unhealthy."

"Mike's a clean cat," said Emily, but Aunt Elizabeth did not look at her.

"Take the child to bed, Laura," she said.

Aunt Laura carried Emily upstairs, helped her un-
dress, and tucked her in. Emily was very sleepy. But
before she was entirely asleep she felt something soft
and purry snuggle against her shoulder. Without letting Elizabeth see her, Aunt Laura had found Mike
and sneaked him in.

Chapter 3

—

*W*ho Will Take Her?

The funeral was held the next morning. The coffin was moved into the parlor, and the Murrays sat around it while the townspeople filed past, staring at the man who lay there. When the service was over, the Murrays stood up and marched around the coffin for their own last look, but Emily pulled back and shook her head.

Douglas Starr was to be buried beside his wife. All the Murrays went, but they left Emily at home. She watched the funeral procession wind up the hill. A light, gray rain was falling, and she was glad of it. It was easier to see Father go away in that gray mist than through sparkling sunshine.

Emily knew the Murrays would be back that afternoon, and they would likely talk about what to do with her. She was not surprised when Ellen came at twilight and said, "You'd better get upstairs, Emily. Your aunts and uncles are coming in here to talk business."

Ellen went back to the kitchen. Emily got up. How could she go to sleep if she didn't know what they had decided? The table in the middle of the room was covered with a heavy cloth that fell to the floor. What luck! In a flash of black stockings, Emily slipped under the cloth. She would hear everything, and nobody would know.

In they came. Emily held her breath. Aunt Eva sighed. At last Uncle Wallace spoke. "What is to be done with the child?"

Aunt Eva whined, "She's so odd. I can't understand her at all."

"I think she has an artistic temperament," said Aunt Laura timidly.

"She's a spoiled child," said Aunt Ruth. "There's work ahead to straighten out her manners."

Emily looked scornfully at Aunt Ruth through the tablecloth.

"I agree," said Aunt Eva, "and I am not prepared to do it."

"Aunt Nancy really should take her," said Uncle

Wallace. "She can afford it better than any of the rest of us."

"Aunt Nancy won't," said Uncle Oliver. "Besides, she's too old. I would like to take Emily, but I really can't. I have a big family already."

"We aren't getting anywhere," Uncle Wallace began again. "She is Juliet's daughter, and some of us must give her a home. I feel Eva isn't strong enough."

"Poor little soul," said Aunt Laura. "Don't you think we might take her, Elizabeth?" she asked.

Aunt Elizabeth moved restlessly. "I don't expect she'd be contented at New Moon with three old people like us."

"I would, I would," thought Emily.

"Ruth, what about you?" asked Uncle Wallace. "You're alone in that big house. It would be good for you to have some company."

"I don't like her," said Aunt Ruth sharply. "She is as sly as a snake."

"With good training, many of her faults could be cured," argued Uncle Wallace.

"I *like* my faults," thought Emily in a rage, "better than your"—she struggled for the right word—"better than your virtues."

"I doubt it," said Aunt Ruth. "As for Douglas Starr, I think it was disgraceful for him to die and leave her without a cent. He was a total failure."

"He wasn't—he wasn't," screamed Emily, sticking her head out from under the tablecloth.

For a moment the Murrays sat as if turned to stone. Then Aunt Ruth stalked to the table and flung aside the cloth. "Come out of that, Em'ly Starr!" commanded Aunt Ruth.

Crimson-cheeked, Emily came out. She was too angry to be scared.

"You shameless little eavesdropper," said Aunt Ruth scornfully. "That's the Starr blood in you; a Murray would *never* do such a thing."

"I wanted to find out what was going to happen to me," cried Emily. "I didn't know it was such a terrible thing to do."

"Your mother would never have done that, Emily," said Aunt Elizabeth sternly.

All the starch went out of Emily at once. She felt guilty and miserable, even though she hadn't known she was doing something wrong.

"Go upstairs," said Aunt Ruth.

Emily went. She was ready to throw herself on her bed and cry when her eyes fell on the old yellow book on her table. A minute later she was writing eagerly with her stubby lead pencil, cheeks flushed and eyes shining. She forgot the Murrays, although she was writing about them. For an hour she wrote, hardly pausing, except to hunt for a word. By the time she heard her relatives coming upstairs, Emily had finished. She felt tired and rather happy. How satisfying it had been to describe Aunt Ruth as ''a dumpy little woman.''

''I wonder what they would say if they knew what I really think of them,'' she murmured as she got into bed.

''Come into the parlor, Emily,'' said Aunt Elizabeth the next morning after breakfast. ''Last night we could not decide who should take you. Cousin Jimmy suggested we draw lots, and that is what we are going to do. Our names are written on these slips of paper. You will draw one, and the person whose name is on it will give you a home.''

Emily trembled. She could not lift her hands.

''Draw,'' said Aunt Elizabeth.

Emily set her teeth and did it. Aunt Elizabeth took the slip from her shaking hand and held it up. On it was her own name, Elizabeth Murray.

"Well, that's settled," said Uncle Wallace. "Of course I'll pay my share of the costs."

"No, thank you," said Aunt Elizabeth. "It is my duty, and I shall do what is needed."

"I am her duty," thought Emily. "Father said nobody ever liked a duty. So Aunt Elizabeth will never like me."

Aunt Laura hugged Emily. "I'm so glad," she said.

Cousin Jimmy told her, "I'll recite my poetry to you. It's very few people I do that for."

Emily was impressed. "Is it hard to write poetry?" she asked.

"It's easy, if you can find enough rhymes," said Cousin Jimmy.

All the other Murrays went home. "We'll pack up here and leave tomorrow," said Aunt Elizabeth.

"How shall I carry my cats?" asked Emily anxiously.

"Cats! You'll take no cats, miss. We have barn cats at New Moon, but no cats in the house."

"Oh, please," cried Emily wildly. "My cats are the only things left in the world that love me. I must take my cats!"

Aunt Elizabeth looked at the child. Why did she— why would anybody want a cat? "You may take *one of your cats,'' she said at last. ''Now, don't argue, Emily. When I say something, I mean it.''

''She does, too,'' said Cousin Jimmy sadly. ''That's the Murray in her. You've got it too, young Emily.''

''But how can I choose between Mike and Saucy Sal?'' cried Emily.

She struggled all day. She loved Mike best, but Ellen liked him too, and Ellen would look after him. Ellen did not like Saucy Sal. It was a bitter decision, but Emily finally decided to leave Mike behind.

''What's this?'' asked Aunt Elizabeth. Emily looked up. Aunt Elizabeth was holding the old yellow book. She was opening it! Emily dashed across and snatched it.

''You mustn't read that, Aunt Elizabeth,'' she cried. ''That's my own private property.''

''Hoity-toity, Miss Starr,'' said Aunt Elizabeth. ''What are you trying to hide? I have a right to read your books. Give it to me!'' Aunt Elizabeth held out her hand.

Emily turned and fled to the kitchen stove. She lifted a cover and crammed her book into the glowing fire. Aunt Elizabeth must never see it, all the things she had written and read to Father, all the things she had said last night about the Murrays. She watched in agony as it blazed and burned, the pages shriveling as if they were alive. A line of writing stood out for a moment. "Aunt Elizabeth is very cold and *hawty*." What if Aunt Elizabeth had seen that?

She could never write those things again, and if she could, she wouldn't dare. She could never write anything again, not if Aunt Elizabeth had to see it. Emily felt as if part of her had died.

Chapter 4

New Moon

They left next morning in a double-seated buggy with a fringed canopy. Emily had never ridden in anything so splendid. Cousin Jimmy and Aunt Elizabeth sat up front, with Aunt Laura and Emily in the seat behind. Emily blinked back tears while Aunt Laura squeezed her hand. They stopped in Charlottetown to eat and shop. "Laura, you and I must get some things for the child," Aunt Elizabeth said.

"Please don't call me 'the child,'" said Emily. "Don't you like my name, Aunt Elizabeth?"

"She can't wear that cheap black dress in Blair Water," Aunt Elizabeth went on, as if Emily had not said a word. "A child of ten shouldn't wear black at all. I shall get her a white dress with black sash for church, and black-and-white check gingham for school. Jimmy, we'll leave the child with you.''

Jimmy took Emily to a restaurant and filled her up with ice cream. Emily had hardly ever eaten ice cream. ''Do you have ice cream at New Moon?'' she asked.

Cousin Jimmy shook his head. ''Your aunt Elizabeth doesn't like newfangled things. We burn candles for light in the house the way they did fifty years ago, though I have everything modern in the barns. New Moon is a pretty good place, Emily. You'll like it there someday.''

It was sunset when they came to New Moon farm. Emily saw a big white house gleaming through tall, ancient trees. She drew a deep breath at the sight of a little dormer window on the roof, and right above it, a real new moon, slender and golden—and there, all of a sudden, was the flash! She was still tingling from it as Cousin Jimmy carried her into the old kitchen, where hams and bunches of herbs hung from the dark rafters, casting strange shadows in the candlelight.

''We'll have supper in the sitting room,'' said Aunt Laura. ''Jimmy will light the fire in there.'' The sitting room was much more cheerful than the kitchen, with diamond-patterned wallpaper and rich red curtains. Emily toasted her toes at the fire and began to enjoy herself.

Aunt Elizabeth brought a mug of milk and two little oatcakes. "Eat your supper, Emily," she said, "and then we'll go up to bed. You are to sleep with me."

Emily shivered. Aunt Elizabeth's bedroom was big and dark. Her high bed had a dark green canopy, a fat duvet, and thick, hard pillows. Aunt Elizabeth waited while Emily changed into her nightgown and said her prayers.

"Aren't you going to open the windows?" asked Emily.

"At night?" Aunt Elizabeth was shocked. "Certainly not!"

Emily lay in the dark beside Aunt Elizabeth. How she longed for her father, and for the stars shining in through her open window! A sob tore her throat, and then another.

"What are you crying for?" asked Aunt Elizabeth. Aunt Elizabeth was just as uncomfortable as Emily. She was used to sleeping by herself. She didn't want Emily in her bed any more than Emily wanted to be there. But Emily was too young for a room of her own, and Laura was not a good sleeper, so Elizabeth had done her duty and taken Emily in with her. And now the ungrateful child was crying! Why?

"I'm homesick, I guess," sobbed Emily. "I'm Fathersick, Aunt Elizabeth. Didn't you feel lonely when *your* father died?"

Aunt Elizabeth had not felt lonely at all. Her father had been a tyrant, and nobody had really been sorry when he died, but she could not say so to Emily. "Stop your tears at once," she said. "I expect you to be grateful and obedient, not a crybaby. What would you have done if you had nobody to take you in? Answer me that!"

"I guess I would have starved to death." Emily had an instant and rather exciting vision of herself lying dead.

"You would have been sent to an orphanage," said Aunt Elizabeth, "and you would have gone hungry there, I can tell you."

"It was good of you to bring me to New Moon," said Emily at once. "I won't bother you long, Aunt Elizabeth. I'll soon be grown up and able to earn my own living."

"The Murray women do not go out to work," said Aunt Elizabeth. "You do not need to think about earning your living. You need to think about being good, and doing everything you should. Now, go to sleep.''

Soon Aunt Elizabeth fell asleep. Emily lay still. How she longed for Saucy Sal! And then she heard the Wind Woman at the window. ''Oh, I'm so glad to hear you,'' Emily whispered. ''I'm not lonesome anymore.''

Next morning Emily found the dairy, where Cousin Jimmy poured pails of foaming milk into big shallow pans and Aunt Laura skimmed off the rich yellow cream.

''You can help Jimmy by driving the cows out to pasture every morning,'' said Aunt Elizabeth.

''Don't be afraid,'' added Aunt Laura. ''The cows know the way. All you have to do is follow them and shut the gates.''

Emily was scared at first. The cows were gigantic! But Aunt Laura was right; they went on their way very quietly, and soon Emily got quite used to them.

''I'll show you my garden,'' Cousin Jimmy offered. ''Elizabeth lets me be in charge of it, because of pushing me down the well.''

''Did she really? *Aunt Elizabeth?*''

''Oh, yes,'' said Jimmy. ''She didn't mean to, of

course. The men were putting a new cover on the well and cleaning it, and we children were playing tag. I made Elizabeth mad, and she went to hit me. I stepped back, and fell in, headfirst. I landed in the mud, but I hit my head on the sides, going down. They thought I was going to die. Poor Elizabeth." Jimmy shook his head. "I got better. Folks say I've never been right in the head since then, but that's because I'm a poet, and because I never worry about anything. Everybody else worries so much they're sure something must be wrong with me."

"Will you recite some of your poetry for me?" asked Emily.

"When the spirit moves me, I will," replied Cousin Jimmy.

"Why don't you write your poetry down?" asked Emily.

"There's not much writing paper at New Moon," said Jimmy. "Elizabeth thinks it's a waste of money. Now come and see my garden."

A high hedge of clipped spruce sheltered the garden. In one corner a sundial of gray stone stood, beyond a walkway edged with conch shells. An old summerhouse filled another corner. "Your great-great-grandfather Murray brought the sundial out from England," said Jimmy. "Finest one in the Maritime Provinces. And Uncle George Murray brought the conchs from the Caribbean. He was a sea captain. Come here when you like,'' he told Emily. ''We'd better go in now, or Elizabeth will give me the Murray look.''

''Aunt Ruth gave me the Murray look,'' said Emily, remembering when she had hidden under the table.

''That was the Ruth Dutton look,'' said Uncle Jimmy. ''Full of spite and malice. The Murray look is different. You'll know it when you see it.''

—

The next day was Sunday. Aunt Elizabeth had decided that Emily would not go to church that week. ''You've got nothing to wear,'' she said. ''Next week your white dress will be ready, but you can't wear that cheap black one to church. You'll have to wear it to school tomorrow, but we'll cover it with an apron.''

Cousin Jimmy showed Emily the Murray graveyard beside the pond. ''Why are all the Murrays buried here?'' asked Emily. ''Are they too good to be buried with everybody else?''

''No, no,'' chuckled Jimmy. ''We aren't as proud as that! When our family came here, there was nothing but woods for miles around, and no roads. That's why the old Murrays are buried here. Do you know the story of how the Murrays came to New Moon?''

''No.''

''They were going to Quebec. It was a rough voyage, and your great-great-grandmother Mary was seasick all the way. The captain was sorry for her, and he said she could go ashore for an hour when they stopped on Prince Edward Island for fresh water. She went, and when she got to shore she said, 'Here I stay.' And that's just what she did. Her husband—Hugh—tried everything, but she would not go back on board that ship. At last he gave in and stayed too.''

''I'm glad,'' said Emily.

''So was Hugh, in the end. He never forgave her, though. Her grave is in that corner. Go and see what he put on it.''

Emily ran over. Under the name and dates was carved only, ''Here I stay.''

Emily shivered. ''I thought the Murrays did not hold a grudge after death,'' she said.

''They don't,'' Jimmy agreed, ''because of this very thing. Folks were horrified, you see.''

''I like this graveyard,'' said Emily, ''but I'm going to be buried in Charlottetown with Father and

Mother. Cousin Jimmy, why is that house over there disappointed?''

''You mean the one that's not finished? Fred Clifford built it for his bride, but she jilted him and married somebody else. Fred moved to British Columbia thirty years ago, but he won't sell the house.''

''And the big gray house?''

''That belongs to Dr. Burnley. He's a good doctor, but he doesn't believe in God. And he's bringing up his daughter the same way, which I think is a shame. Ilse Burnley is a great girl, Emily, with golden hair and eyes like yellow diamonds.''

''Doesn't her mother teach her things?''

''Her mother is—dead,'' said Cousin Jimmy, with an odd little pause.

Chapter 5

*T*rial by Fire

Aunt Elizabeth drove Emily to school the next morning, introduced her to the teacher, whose name was Miss Brownell, and drove away. Much against her will, Emily wore a coverall apron and a sunbonnet. They had belonged to her mother when she was a girl, and were hopelessly out of date. The other children stared and whispered. ''Miss Pridey,'' hissed a beady-eyed girl across the aisle. Emily could not hold back her tears.

''What is the matter with you, Emily?'' demanded the teacher. ''Why are you crying?''

Emily could not answer.

''You will stay in at recess,'' said Miss Brownell angrily.

At lunchtime, however, Emily had to go outside. She faced a crowd of unfriendly faces. Emily was a stranger and one of the proud Murrays, two counts against her, and her clothes were all wrong. "You may have buttoned boots," said Beady-eyes, "but you are living on charity."

"Look at the baby apron," laughed another girl, tossing her brown curls.

"Your cousin Jimmy is an idiot," said a third tormenter.

"He isn't," cried Emily. "You may say nasty things about me, but you can't insult my family. Why don't you like me?"

"Because you ain't like us," muttered Brown Curls.

"I wouldn't want to be," said Emily. She marched away.

The afternoon went better, even though the teacher made fun of Emily's spelling. All the girls giggled except one who had not been at school that morning. She was as unlike the others as Emily herself, but in a different way. She wore a long, faded dress, and was barefoot. Her thick, short hair was fluffed out around her head like a golden bush; her glowing eyes were light brown. She had a large mouth and a firm chin. She was the only girl the teacher did not make fun of. Emily was fascinated.

At recess one of the girls came up to Emily with a

box in her hand. "Here is a present for you," she said with a friendly smile.

Emily smiled back. She opened the box and looked inside. Then she screamed and flung it away. There was a snake in the box. Emily trembled. The girls giggled. "I hate you all," cried Emily.

"If you come to school tomorrow," said Beady-eyes, "we'll put that snake around your neck."

"No you won't," cried the girl with the golden hair.

"Ilse Burnley, this isn't your business," said Beady-eyes.

"Don't sass me, Piggy." Ilse shook her fist. "Now, you pick up that snake and throw it in the trash." Ilse faced the others. "Leave Emily alone," she said. "If you don't, I'll slit your throats and tear out your eyes and cut off your ears."

The others slunk away. Ilse turned to Emily. "They're jealous," she said. "You smack their faces if they give you a hard time." She vaulted the fence and ran off into the maple bush.

"I hope you're not mad at me, Emily," said the girl who had given her the box. "I didn't know there was a snake in that box. The others told me it was a present. I really like you, Emily." Rhoda Stuart was pretty and popular. Emily wanted to believe her.

"I'll ask the teacher to let you sit with me," Rhoda said. "We come from the two best families in town, so we should sit together. I'm having a birthday party the first week in July, and I'm going to invite you. I'm not inviting Ilse Burnley, though."

"Don't you like her?"

"No. She's a tomboy. Her father doesn't believe in God, and she doesn't either. Isn't it awful, the way she does her hair? You have such a high forehead, Emily, you'd be beautiful if you had bangs."

Emily rushed home to ask. "No, you can't have bangs," said Aunt Elizabeth. "At New Moon, the only creatures with bangs are the cows!" She laughed.

Emily sighed. But she had another question. "Why doesn't Ilse Burnley's father believe in God?"

"Because of what her mother did," said Cousin Jimmy. Aunt Elizabeth glared at him, and Emily knew he would not tell her anything more about it.

After a few days Emily began to enjoy school, even though she did not get along with Miss Brownell. The other girls stopped making fun of her as soon as they found out she was much better at making fun of them. Rhoda was her chum. "Your aunt's rich, isn't she?" she asked. "Is she going to give you music lessons?"

"I don't know," said Emily uncomfortably.

"She's got an awful temper, hasn't she?" asked Rhoda.

"No," cried Emily.

"Yes, she does," said Rhoda. "She nearly killed your cousin Jimmy when he was little. Your father was poor as a church mouse, wasn't he?"

"My father was a very rich man," said Emily quietly. "People don't need money to be rich."

"I think they do," said Rhoda. "But my mother says Elizabeth Murray will likely leave you all her money when she dies, so I don't care if you are living on charity, I still love you, Emily." Ilse Burnley did not appear after that first day. Rhoda said Ilse only came to school when she wanted to.

Emily could have been happy if only she had had paper to write on. She ached for the old yellow book, missing what she had written there, as well as the blank pages. But fate was getting ready to help her, and to help her on her darkest day.

That day Miss Brownell had read a poem to some of the older students. Emily was supposed to be doing arithmetic, but the glory of the "Bugle Song" caught her, and when Miss Brownell got to the "horns of elf-land faintly blowing," Emily rushed forward, crying, "Oh, Teacher, read it again!"

Miss Brownell shut her book and shut her lips and gave Emily a furious slap on the face. "Mind your own business, Emily Starr," she snapped.

Emily had never been slapped in her life. She went home in shame and misery, but did not dare say anything. Aunt Elizabeth would say Miss Brownell was right, and Aunt Laura would be hurt because Emily had behaved badly and been punished. Emily's stomach churned. She could not choke down a mouthful of dinner.

Then fate stepped in. Aunt Laura took Emily to the big bookcase to show her an old sewing box, a Murray heirloom. Inside was a big, flat bundle of dusty paper, deep pink in color. "It's time this old paper was burned," Aunt Laura said. "It's just forms, from when Father had the post office here."

"Oh, Aunt Laura," Emily gasped, "please, *please,* give them to me."

"Why, child?" asked her aunt. "What on earth can you do with them?"

"Oh, Aunty, they have such lovely blank backs for writing on. It would be a sin to burn that paper."

"You can have them, dear. Only don't let Elizabeth see them."

"I won't," breathed Emily.

She gathered the precious bundle and ran upstairs

to the dormer room. Fluffy balls of wool hung from the walls, and sometimes Aunt Laura came to spin it into yarn, but usually Emily had the room to herself. She took one of the pink forms, got a stub of pencil from her pocket, and began, "Dear Father."

That night the chickens were not fed, and Cousin Jimmy had to fetch the cows himself. Emily wrote until it was too dark to see. By that time she did not hate Miss Brownell any longer. She felt empty and content. She folded the old forms and wrote on the outside, "To Mr. Douglas Starr," then hid the precious bundle on a low shelf behind the old sofa.

From that time onward, Emily wrote a letter to her father almost every night. She told him about Rhoda and the birthday party, about New Moon and her relatives there, and about Ilse Burnley. She wrote:

I'd like to get akwanted with Ilse, but Rhoda says I mustn't have any chum but her or she will cry her eyes out. Good night, my beloved Father.

> Your most obedient humble servant,
> Emily B. Starr

Chapter 6

*F*rom Rhoda to Ilse

Rhoda was going to have an enormous birthday cake with pink icing and ten tall pink candles, and the party invitations, written on pink, gilt-edged paper, were being sent through the mail! Emily was Rhoda's best friend; she was sure to get one. Other girls thought she might persuade Rhoda to invite them. Jennie Strang even tried to bribe her with a pencil case, which Emily refused rather grandly. It was fun to feel important to others as well as to herself.

Then suddenly everything changed. On the first Sunday in July, Rhoda came to Sunday school with a fat girl in a fancy blue silk dress, white lace stockings, and bangs that came down to her eyes. Emily was ignored. She sat beside Jennie. "Who's the new girl?" she whispered.

"Muriel Porter," Jennie answered. "She's

here for the summer. Her family is rich, and she comes from the city, so Rhoda thinks she's wonderful.''

''Rhoda's not like that,'' protested Emily.

''She is too,'' said Jennie. ''I'm glad I'm not invited to her silly party.''

Emily was shocked. ''How do you know?''

''The invitations went out yesterday. Didn't you get yours?''

''No-o-o.''

Emily wondered, and worried a little. She went to the post office herself on Monday, but there was no pink envelope for her, and none on Tuesday either. ''So you're not invited after all,'' said Jennie.

''No,'' admitted Emily bitterly.

''I think it's mean,'' said Jennie, ''after all the fuss she's made over you. But that's Rhoda.''

''Perhaps it's a mistake,'' said Emily loyally.

Jennie stared. ''Don't you know? Muriel Porter hates you. She said she wouldn't come if you were there, and Rhoda was so wild to have Muriel she promised she wouldn't invite you.''

''Muriel Porter doesn't even know me.''

''She has a crush on Rhoda's brother Fred, so Fred teased her. He said you were the sweetest girl in Blair Water, and he wants you for his girl when you're older. Anyway, Rhoda is deceitful. She told you she didn't know about the snake in the box, and it was her idea in the first place.''

Emily was crushed. The blow was so bitter that she could not even write about it to her father.

Next Sunday Rhoda was alone. Muriel Porter had gone home because her father was ill, and Rhoda smiled at Emily as if nothing had changed. Emily turned away. Rhoda had betrayed her. Emily was sure she would never love or trust anyone ever again.

The feeling poisoned everything. Emily was sure that all the girls were making fun of her. She didn't feel like eating, and she lost weight. Aunt Elizabeth decided Emily's long hair must be too heavy for her in the heat of summer. ''I'm sure that's why you've been miserable lately,'' she told the girl. ''I'm going to shingle your hair. Wait here while I get my scissors.''

''Don't cut it *all* off,'' Emily begged. ''It's my one beauty.''

Emily waited helplessly. Father had been so proud of her hair. Aunt Elizabeth came back. The scissors clicked as she opened them. At the sound, Emily felt her brows drawing together. She felt a strange energy. ''Aunt Elizabeth,'' she said, ''*my hair is not going to be cut off.* Let me hear no more of this.''

Aunt Elizabeth turned pale. She put down the scissors, turned away, and fled to the kitchen. "I saw Father looking out of the child's face," she gasped to Laura. "And she said, 'Let me hear no more of this'—his very words."

Emily ran to the mirror. The strange feeling was vanishing, but she caught a glimpse of it, the Murray look, she supposed. She shivered, but somehow she knew her hair would not be cut.

From that day Emily was herself again. She did not grieve any longer over her lost friendship. Life was good, except that Emily was afraid Aunt Elizabeth would get even somehow for being scared.

She was right. A week later, against orders, Emily went barefoot to the store. On the way back, she composed her third poem, "To a Buttercup." The first two verses came easily, but then Emily was stuck. By the time she had found the right ending, she was home. Aunt Elizabeth looked at her bare feet and locked her in the spare room for punishment.

Emily was terrified of the big, dark room with its huge, canopied bed. Generations of Murrays had died in that bed, so Cousin Jimmy had said, and Emily was sure that something horrible was waiting to jump out at her from behind its dark curtains.

Aunt Elizabeth turned the key. "You'll stay there

until bedtime,'' she said. ''Let it be a lesson to you not to disobey me again.''

In the shadows, something moved. Emily bit back a scream. Suddenly a ray of sunlight came through a slit in the blinds and lit up the picture of her grandfather that hung above the mantel. The old man seemed to be glaring right at Emily! In panic, she rushed to the window and pulled up the blind.

A ladder leaned against the window. Emily shoved up the window, climbed through, and backed down the shaky wooden rungs. When she reached the bottom, she ran into the woods and did not stop until she reached the end of the path.

There she found Ilse Burnley.

''Where are you running to?'' asked Ilse.

''I'm running away,'' said Emily. ''I disobeyed Aunt Elizabeth, but it wasn't fair of her to shut me in that horrible room.'' She told Ilse the whole story.

''You're a brave little cuss,'' said Ilse.

Emily gasped at Ilse's language, but she was glad Ilse thought she was brave.

''You'd better come home with me,'' said Ilse. ''There's a thunderstorm coming.''

The Burnley house was a mess. Nothing was in its right place, and a thick layer of dust lay over everything. It was a great place to play. You didn't have to be careful not to mess things up. Ilse and Emily played hide-and-seek until the thunder got too heavy and the lightning too bright for Emily.

"Aren't you afraid of thunder?" she asked Ilse.

"No, I ain't afraid of anything except the devil," answered Ilse.

"I thought you didn't believe in the devil," said Emily.

"Father says there's a devil, all right," said Ilse. "It's only God he doesn't believe in. If there is a devil, and no God to keep him down, then I'm right to be scared, or that's what I think. Look here, Emily, I like you heaps. I knew you'd soon get sick of Rhoda, that white-livered, lying sneak. I'd go to school regular if I could sit with you."

"All right," said Emily.

"You won't be ashamed of me because my clothes are queer and I don't believe in God?"

"No. But if you knew Father's God, you'd believe in *Him*."

"I wouldn't. Besides, I don't like talking about God," said Ilse. "Emily, please like me. Nobody else does."

"Your father must like you," said Emily.

"He doesn't." Ilse was positive. "Sometimes he

hates the sight of me. I wish he did like me. I'm going to be an elo-cu-tion-ist when I grow up.''

''What's that?''

''A woman who recites poetry at concerts. I can do it dandy. What are you going to be?''

''A poetess.''

''Golly!'' said Ilse. ''Can you write poetry?''

Emily proudly recited her buttercup poem.

''Emily Byrd Starr, you didn't make that up out of your own head!''

''I did too.''

''Well, I guess you're a real poetess all right.''

It was a proud moment for Emily. But now it was getting dark, and she had to go home. She trotted happily along the path, but when she reached home, the ladder was gone! Emily crept in through the kitchen door. This time she was lucky. Aunt Laura was alone. ''Emily, where did you come from?'' she asked. ''I was just going to let you out. Elizabeth has gone to prayer meeting, and she said I could.''

Aunt Laura gave Emily a big cookie and let her feed Saucy Sal a whole cup of scraps. ''I suppose I disgraced the Murrays by going barefoot,'' Emily said.

''Don't let Elizabeth see you another time,'' said

Aunt Laura. "What she doesn't know won't hurt her."

"I ought to obey her," said Emily, "because she's the head of the family. Aunt Laura, Ilse Burnley and I are going to be chums."

"Poor Ilse," sighed Aunt Laura.

"Why doesn't her father like her? It's terrible!"

"He does like her, really. He only thinks he doesn't."

"Why does he think it?"

"You are too young to understand, Emily."

Emily was sure she could understand, if only Aunt Laura explained carefully, but she knew Aunt Laura would not even try.

Chapter 7

The Tansy Patch

Emily and Ilse had been friends for two weeks before they had their first fight. They were making a playhouse in the woods. Emily wanted a parlor. Ilse didn't. "You little sniveling chit," she screamed, "don't think you're going to boss me just because you live at New Moon."

"I'm not going to boss you," said Emily, with crimson cheeks. "I'm not going to play with you ever again."

"I'm glad to be rid of you, you stuck-up *biped*," cried Ilse. "If I couldn't write better poetry than you, I'd hang myself."

"I'll lend you a dime to buy the rope," snapped Emily. She marched away, leaving Ilse to knock down the playhouse walls and kick the moss garden to pieces. After Emily had cooled down, she went to the dormer room and cried. She had lost another chum.

The next morning Emily went back to the playhouse to pick up her share of the broken china and boards. The walls were back in place, the moss garden remade, and a beautiful parlor had been connected to the living room by a spruce arch.

"What kept you?" asked Ilse cheerfully. "I hope you like your parlor."

"I thought you'd never be my friend again," said Emily.

"That was yesterday!" said Ilse.

Ilse was like that, flying into rages and being cheerful and loving in between them. "I've got Dad's temper," she said. "Wait till you see him in a rage!"

Dr. Burnley was kind and gentle to anybody who was sick, though he was often rude to people who were not. Through the whole of July, he had been trying to save Teddy Kent's life up at the Tansy Patch. Teddy was getting better at last, but not quickly enough. One day Dr. Burnley stopped Ilse and Emily with their fishing poles on the way to the pond and ordered them to go and play with Teddy Kent.

Ilse did not want to go, but Emily did. Emily had

only seen Teddy once before he got ill, but she thought he was very handsome, with his dark brown hair and black-browed blue eyes.

"Teddy's nice, but his mother is strange," Ilse told her on their way to the Tansy Patch. "She never goes out, not even to church. I guess it's because of the scar on her face. They haven't lived here long."

Mrs. Kent was a tiny woman with mournful eyes. She would have been pretty except for the scar that slanted across her cheeks. She and Teddy lived in a tiny, neglected house on top of a hill overgrown with tansy. Wild rosebushes covered the shaky rail fence. The gate sagged.

Teddy was glad to see the girls, and they all had a happy afternoon, at the end of which Teddy's eyes were brighter and his cheeks had some color in them. Mrs. Kent saw that the visit had been good for him. She was eager for the girls to come again, and they did so almost every day throughout August.

Sometimes Teddy took them to the barn loft and showed them his drawings. In the evening they sat on the veranda steps while Teddy and Ilse sang, or Ilse recited, or Emily told stories. Mrs. Kent never joined them, though Emily was sure she watched and listened, hidden behind the kitchen blind.

Aunt Elizabeth allowed Emily to go to the Tansy Patch, but only because Dr. Burnley had ordered it.

"Teddy is a very nice boy, Father," Emily wrote in one of the letters that were piling up on the shelf behind the sofa in the dormer room.

He is going to be a famus artist some day. He keeps his pictures in the barn loft because his mother doesn't like to see them. Teddy won't pet the cats because his mother gets upset and says he likes them better than her. He's afraid she might even hurt the cats. I thought Aunt Elizabeth was tirannical, but Mrs. Kent is worse, except that she loves Teddy and Aunt Elizabeth does not love me.

Mrs. Kent does not like Ilse or me. I believe she is jellus of us because Teddy likes us. Mrs. Kent is a very misterious person, like some people you read about in books. I like misterious people but not too close.

Aunt Elizabeth and Aunt Laura both approve of my friendship with Ilse. I am glad because they do not often approve of the same thing. I am getting used to fighting with Ilse now, and I don't mind it so much. We make up right away. Yesterday Ilse called me a lousy lizard and a toothless viper. I don't call names because that is unladylike but I smile and that makes Ilse far madder than if I scowled like her.

Dear Father, I am happy here. It isn't wrong to be happy, is it? I have got akwanted with Lofty John. Ilse is a great friend of his and often goes to watch him working in his carpenter shop. I go with her, even though I know he is an enemy of my family because he wouldn't sell Aunt Elizabeth the land behind New Moon when she asked him to. He is very polite to me, but I don't always like him. When I ask him a serious question, he always winks over my head when he answers. That is insulting.

School begins again next week. Ilse is going to ask Miss Brownell if I can sit with her. Teddy is going too, even though his mother does not like the idea. Aunt Laura says the right way to end a letter to a friend is yours affeckshunately.

So I am yours very affeckshunately,
Emily Byrd Starr

Chapter   8

$\mathcal{P}$erry Miller Comes to New Moon

Emily had wanted to explore Mr. James Lee's pasture ever since Cousin Jimmy had told her the dreadful story about the old well. Two brothers, Silas and Thomas Lee, owned the property and had the well dug. It was a very deep well. The diggers went down ninety feet before they found water, and they lined the well with rocks to keep the sides from falling in. Then the brothers started fighting about what the well house should look like, and Silas bashed Thomas with his hammer. Thomas died, and Silas went to prison and died there. Mr. James Lee's father inherited the property, and decided to move the house. The old well was covered with planks.

Emily had never gone to look for the well because Mr. James Lee kept his bull in the pasture, and she was frightened of the animal. One Saturday, however, she did not see the bull anywhere, and climbed the fence. It was not difficult to find the old well. Emily dragged a board off it, and knelt on another board to look down.

There wasn't much to see. Over the years, ferns had grown out from the rocks, hiding the depths. Emily pulled the board back and stood up. There, not twenty feet away, was the bull, coming toward her.

Emily stood there. She might have reached the fence if she had turned and run immediately, but she could not move. Then suddenly a boy tore past her and threw a stone at the bull's nose. The huge animal bellowed and turned to follow the boy. "Run now," he screamed, but Emily still did not run. She watched, making sure the boy reached the fence ahead of the bull. Only then did she turn. The bull, missing one target, was after her again, and she only just managed to scramble to safety. She was still trembling when she met the boy who had rescued her at the corner of the fence.

"Thank you," she said shyly, looking up at him from under her long lashes.

"Isn't he something," said the boy easily, staring at her.

"He's dreadful," shivered Emily, "and I was so scared."

"Really?" said the boy. "You didn't look scared, standing there. What's your name?"

"Emily Byrd Starr."

"Live around here?"

"I live at New Moon."

"I'm going to be the new chore boy at New Moon," said the boy. "I wasn't going to, but now I am. Simple Jimmy Murray was around last week, talking to my old beast of an aunt Tom."

"He isn't simple," said Emily indignantly.

"Maybe not; I don't know him," said the boy.

"And you should not call your aunt an old beast."

"I don't know what else to call her. She's not a young beast," said the boy. "Want to know my name?"

"Of course."

"It's Perry Miller. I guess you go to school."

"Yes, don't you?"

"Never did yet, but now I guess I will."

"Can't you read and write?"

"I can read some, and figger. Dad learned me some when he was alive. Dad was a sea captain, and I useter sail with him. I figgered on going to sea myself, but now I plan to get an eddicashun. If I go to school I'll learn like thunder. I suppose you're very clever."

"I don't know. I do write poetry."

"Then I'll write poetry too."

"Maybe you can't. Teddy Kent can't write poetry, and he's very clever."

"Who's Teddy Kent?"

"A friend of mine."

"Then I'll punch him in the face," said Perry.

"You won't!" Emily turned angrily away and started toward home. Perry fell in beside her.

"I guess I'll go to New Moon now and fix it up about being the chore boy," he said. "I won't punch anybody if you don't want me to, but you have to like me too."

"Of course I'll like you," said Emily.

Two days later Perry Miller was chore boy at New Moon. Emily wrote to her father about him.

He's head of his class already at school. I am helping him learn to speak properly. Teddy doesn't like him much.

I am sorry winter has come, because now we can't play outside. I don't like going to the Tansy

Patch, because Mrs. Kent sits and watches us all the time, so we don't go much, only when Teddy begs us.

Aunt Elizabeth had a big fight with Lofty John, and it's my fault. I ate a lot of apples at his workshop, and then he told me they were poisoned. Aunt Elizabeth ran for the doctor, but Lofty John was only joking. My stomak hurt because I ate too many apples, not because I was dying. "I told Lofty John what I thought of him," said Aunt Elizabeth, "and Emily, you deserve your stomak ake." She was right. I am sorry I ever went near an enemy of New Moon.

Ilse was here on Sunday and we went up in the garret and talked about God, because that is propper on Sundays. Ilse is very curious about God, even though she doesn't believe in Him. She spells his name with a capital G now because it is best to be on the safe side. I think God is just like my flash, only my flash only lasts a second, and God lasts always.

> Goodnight, my dearest of fathers,
> Emily

Chapter 9

Check for Miss Brownell

Emily and Ilse were sitting on the side bench in
the schoolroom. Ilse had asked if they could,
and Miss Brownell had said yes, although she
still disliked Emily and often made fun of her.
The side bench was everybody's favorite. You
could see all over the school without turning
your head, and Miss Brownell could not sneak
up behind you. It was the view from the window that Emily loved; she could look out at the
spruces where the Wind Woman played, at the
red squirrels running along the fence, and far in
the distance, beyond the Blair Water valley, she
could glimpse the snow-covered sand hills and
the deep dark blue of the ocean.

Emily had totally forgotten that she was supposed to be doing fractions. She was writing a
poem about the view, and was so deeply lost in

her writing that she did not see Miss Brownell stepping softly toward her. Ilse was drawing a picture on her slate, or she would have warned Emily.

"I suppose you have finished your sums, Emily?" Miss Brownell drew Emily's slate out of her hand and held it up high. "What is this?" she sneered " 'Lines on the View—spelled "v-e-w"—from the Window of Blair Water School.' Children, we seem to have a budding poet here."

Emily shuddered. Nothing was more terrible than the thought of mean, petty Miss Brownell reading her precious poetry. "P-Please don't read it, Miss Brownell," she stammered. "It's nothing. I'll rub it off. I'll do my sums right away."

Miss Brownell laughed cruelly. "This isn't nothing, Emily. It is a whole slateful of—*poetry*. Think of that, children—*poetry*. And Emily doesn't want us to read it? How selfish she is."

Most of the children giggled, Rhoda loudest of all. Miss Brownell held up Emily's slate and read the poem through her nose in a singsong way. " 'Vistas in some fairy dream'," she chanted, shutting her eyes and wagging her head from side to side. The children's giggles turned to shouts of laughter. Rhoda raised her hand.

"Please, Miss Brownell," she said, "Emily has a

whole bunch of poetry in her desk. She was reading
it to Ilse Burnley this morning when she was supposed to be doing history."

Perry Miller turned, and a spitball hit Rhoda's
face, but Miss Brownell got to Emily's desk a step
ahead of Emily and seized the "bunch of poetry."

"Don't touch them—you have no *right*!" gasped
Emily. She had written the poems at recess when it
was too stormy to go outside, and had meant to take
them home that night. And now this horrible woman
was going to read them to the whole school!

Miss Brownell flipped through the precious papers. " 'Lines on a Birch Tree'—looks more like
lines on a very dirty piece of paper, Emily. 'Lines to
My Favorite Cat'—a romantic *tail,* I suppose. 'The
Violets Spell'—I hope the violet *spells* better than
you do, Emily. 'Lines composed on the bank of Blair
Water gazing at the stars—

'Crusted with uncounted gems,
Those stars so distant, cold and true,'

Don't try to pass those lines off as your own, Emily.
You couldn't have written them."

"I did—I did!" Emily was white with outrage.

"We have wasted enough time over this trash,"

said Miss Brownell. "Go to your seat, Emily." She crumpled the papers and moved toward the stove. Just as she opened the stove door, Emily caught at the papers and tore them from her hand.

"You shall not have them," she gasped, the Murray look blazing from her face. It did not have quite the same impact on Miss Brownell as on Aunt Elizabeth, but the teacher stepped back all the same.

"I am coming to New Moon tonight to tell your aunt Elizabeth about this," she said.

Emily was thrilled about saving her precious poems, but her excitement died quickly. As soon as she got home, she ran to the garret and hid her poems; then she sat at the window and waited. At last Miss Brownell came striding up the lane.

Long minutes passed before Aunt Laura came to summon Emily. Aunt Elizabeth sat stiffly by the kitchen table. Miss Brownell sat in the rocking chair, her pale eyes glittering with triumph.

"I am sorry to say," said Aunt Elizabeth, "that I have been hearing some very bad things about you, Emily."

"No," said Emily, "I don't think you are sorry."

"Such impertinence!" said Miss Brownell. "You see what I have to put up with."

"I don't mean to be impertinent," Emily continued, "but you are not sorry. You are angry because I have disgraced New Moon, but you are a little glad that Miss Brownell agrees with you that I am bad."

"I am ashamed of you," said Aunt Elizabeth.

"It was not as bad as you think, Aunt Elizabeth," said Emily. "You see—"

"Be quiet," said Aunt Elizabeth. "I have heard the whole story."

"You heard a pack of lies," said Perry suddenly, sticking his head down from the kitchen loft. Everybody jumped.

"Perry Miller, come down here at once," ordered Aunt Elizabeth.

"Can't," replied Perry.

"At once," repeated Aunt Elizabeth.

"All right, if I must." Perry swung bare legs down from the loft. Aunt Laura shrieked. "I've just got my wet duds off," said Perry cheerfully, "fell into the brook when I was watering the cows. Was going to put on dry ones, but just as you say—"

"Perry, get your clothes on immediately," ordered Cousin Jimmy. Perry's legs disappeared again, and he chuckled.

Aunt Elizabeth stood and turned angrily to Emily. "Emily, kneel down here before Miss Brownell and beg her pardon," she commanded.

Emily's pale cheeks turned bright red. Miss Brownell smiled. This was victory! Emily would be ashamed forever. Miss Brownell knew it. Emily knew it. But Emily did not kneel.

"Aunt Elizabeth, *please* let me tell my side of the story."

"I have heard enough," said Aunt Elizabeth. "Do as I say."

Cousin Jimmy stared at the ceiling. "A human being should not kneel to anyone but God," he said.

Elizabeth Murray stood very still, looking at him. "Emily," she said at last, "I was wrong. I won't ask you to kneel. But you must apologize to your teacher."

"I am sorry for anything I did that was wrong," said Emily carefully, "and I ask your pardon for it."

Miss Brownell could happily have shaken "simple Jimmy Murray." She glared at Emily. "See you behave yourself in future," she said.

Emily ate bread and milk in the pantry that night, while the others supped on New Moon sausages. They smelled wonderful, but Emily hardly missed them. She was writing her next poem in her head when Aunt Laura came in at last with ginger cookies.

Chapter 10

Letters to Father

Dear Father:

I am a *famus heroine!*

Ilse asked me to stay all night because her father wouldn't be home till very late. So I asked Aunt Elizabeth, even though I hardly dared hope, and she said Yes! Later I heard her talking to Aunt Laura in the pantry and she said, It is a shame the way the doctor leaves that poor child so much alone at nights. And Aunt Laura said The poor man is warped. He was not like that before his wife—and then Aunt Elizabeth said s-s-s-h, little pitchers have big ears. I knew she meant me. I wish I could find out what Ilse's mother did. It worrys me after I go to bed. Ilse has no idea. Once she asked her father and he told her never to mention *that woman* again. Another thing that worrys me is Silas Lee who killed his brother at the old well. How dreadful he must have felt!

I went to Ilse's and we played in the garret. I like this in the daytime, I said, but it must be awful queer at night. Mice, said Ilse—and spiders, and gosts. Nonsense, I said, but it did feel queer. It's easy to talk, said Ilse. I bet you wouldn't stay up here alone at night. I wouldn't mind it a bit, I said. Then I dare you to do it, said Ilse. I dare you to sleep here all night. Then I saw I was in an awful skrape Father dear. I was a fool to bost. If I didn't do it, Ilse would remind me every time we fought, and she'd tell Teddy and he'd think I am a coward. So I said I'll do it Ilse Burnley and I'm not afraid. (But oh I was—inside.) We dragged out an old feather bed and Ilse gave me a pillow. It was dark by then and Ilse wouldn't go up with me. I got into bed and blew out the lamp, but I couldnt go to sleep. The moonlight made the garret look weerd. I dont know exactly what weerd means but I feel the garret was it. At last I heard the doctor driving in and then I felt better and before long I went to sleep and I had a terrible dream. I dreamed a big newspaper came and chased me, and then it was on fire and just as it caught me I woke up and I smelled smoke and it was coming from the rag room and I could see firelight under the door. I yelled and tore down to Ilses room and she woke her father and then all three of us ran up and down the garret stairs with pails of water and we made an awful mess but we got the fire out. Whew said the doctor a few minutes later would have been too late. I put on a fire when I came in and a spark must have got out. I see a hole in the plaster. How did you diskover the fire Emily. I was sleeping in the garret I said. What in—*what* were you doing there. Ilse dared me I said. You little devil, said the doctor. I suppose it is awful to be called a devil, but it sounded like a complement. Yesterday the Shrewsbury *Weekly Times* came, and the story was there how the fire was diskovered in time by Miss Emily Starr!

MAY 20.

Yesterday was my birthday dear Father. It will soon be a year since I came to New Moon. I feel as if I had always lived here. I have grown two inches. Cousin Jimmy measured me. Aunt Laura made me a lovely cake and she gave me her pink satin brokade. What will you do with that asked Ilse. Ill keep it with my treasures and look at it because its beautiful I said. Aunt Elizabeth gave me a dixonary. That was a useful present but when Im writing something I get so exited I hate to stop to hunt up a word to see how it is spelled. Cousin Jimmy gave me a big thick blank book. It will be so nice to write pieces in. But I will still use the old letter-bills to write to you, dear Father, because I can fold them up and address them like real letters. Teddy gave me a picture of myself. Perry gave me a young hen, and I can sell all her eggs. Ilse gave me a box of candy.

JUNE 1.

Dear Father:

I wrote my first letter today, I mean my first letter to go in the mail. It was to Great-aunt Nancy who lives at Priest Pond. Write a nice letter said Aunt Elizabeth and I will read it over.

JUNE 7.

Great-aunt Nancy wrote Aunt Elizabeth that I must be a very stupid child to write such a stupid letter. I felt insulted because I am not stupid. I could not write an interesting letter when Aunt Elizabeth was going to read it.

Teddy and Perry and Ilse and I play we are

living in the days of knights and ladies. Sometimes we play at the Tansy Patch. I have a queer feeling that Teddy's mother hates me this summer. Last summer she just didn't like me. The cats are not there now. Teddy is sure his mother got rid of them because she thought he liked them too much.

JUNE 14.

"We have composition in school now. Today I learned that you put in things like this " " when you write what somebody said, and after a question a mark like this ? and when a letter is left out a mark like a comma in the air. Miss Brownell is mean but she does teach you things. I want to be fair even if I do hate her. I like writing about people I don't like. Aunt Laura is nicer to live with than Aunt Elizabeth, but Aunt Elizabeth is nicer to write about. I can deskribe her fawlts, but I feel wikked if I say anything unkind about dear Aunt Laura.

> Your lovingest daughter,
> Emily B. Starr

Chapter 11

New Moon in Danger

In September word came to New Moon that Lofty John had decided to cut down his grove. The magnificent stand of trees would be destroyed, and with it, the beauty of New Moon. Emily and Ilse's playhouse would be gone. Cousin Jimmy's beloved garden would wither and die when the cold north winds blew and there were no trees left to protect his tender plants. Laura went around sighing.

"I've got an idea," said Teddy, trying to be helpful. "Lofty John is a Catholic. Don't Catholics have to do what the priest tells them? If your Aunt Elizabeth goes to Father Cassidy, won't he tell Lofty John not to cut down the grove?"

"Aunt Elizabeth won't go," said Emily. "She's too proud."

"Not even to save the trees? Not even to save New Moon?"

"No."

Emily wondered if she could go to Father Cassidy herself. It was a frightening thought. Her own family, like most of the people in Blair Water, was Protestant. Emily had never even seen a Catholic priest. But Aunt Elizabeth was right. If New Moon was ruined, it would be her fault.

Emily went outside after supper and turned up the hill leading to the parish house. Perhaps Father Cassidy wouldn't see her. Maybe he only talked to Catholics. Maybe he was out. Emily drew a deep breath. Then she knocked on the door, and the maid led her into a book-lined study. On top of one of the bookcases lay the most enormous cat Emily had ever seen, totally black. It stared down at her. What must the priest be like, when he had a cat like this? Emily shivered.

And then in came Father Cassidy, with the friendliest smile in the world. He was a big man, brown as a nut. He shook hands and bent to look at her ears. "Pointed ears!" he said. "It's an elf that's come to visit me. Sit down, and tell me all the news from fairyland."

Emily would have liked nothing better, but her

errand was too important. "I'm only Emily Starr from New Moon," she said, "and I'm a Protestant." She looked at Father Cassidy. Would he send her away now that he knew?

"So you are," he said, "and I'm sorry about that. The woods around here are full of Protestants, but I haven't seen an elf for a hundred years."

Emily stared at him. He didn't look a hundred years old. "You are a kind of minister, aren't you?" she asked.

"Kind av," he agreed. "Now, what's bothering you?"

"Please help me, Father Cassidy," said Emily. "I'm in dreadful trouble." She told him the story.

"Humph," said Father Cassidy when she had finished. "I can hardly use the power av the Church to stop a man from doing what he wants with his own property."

Emily's eyes overflowed.

"Come now, darlin', don't cry," Father Cassidy begged her. "Elves don't cry. I think I can make Lofty John change his mind. He's a friend av mine. I'll put it to him, as man to man, that no decent Irishman carries on a fight with women, and that no sensible man would destroy a grove of fine old trees for the sake of a grudge. Yes, Emily, I think you can count on it, those trees will not be cut down.''

Emily felt a flood of joy. ''I can never thank you enough,'' she said.

''That's true,'' said Father Cassidy, ''so have a piece of cake and tell me about yourself.''

Emily was hungry. She also had another problem. In the long poem she was writing, the heroine was shut up in a convent. Emily wanted to get her out, but not knowing anything about nuns and convents, did not know how. Father Cassidy listened again. ''You need a dispensation from the Pope,'' he said at last.

'' 'Dispensation' is a hard word to put into a poem,'' said Emily, ''but I'll manage.''

''I'm sure av it,'' said Father Cassidy. ''Have you written any other poetry?''

''Oh, yes,'' said Emily, and recited her latest, ''Evening Dreams.'' It had seemed wonderful to her when she wrote it, but now she was sure it was no good.

Father Cassidy sat silently. The poem *wasn't* very good, but there was one good line in it. ''Keep on writing poetry,'' he said at last. ''You'll be able to do something by and by—I don't know how much, but keep on—keep on.''

Emily was so happy she wanted to cry. It was the first time anyone but her father had praised her work. "Aunt Elizabeth scolds me for writing poetry," she said.

"Of course," Father Cassidy replied. "Have another piece of cake."

"No, thank you," said Emily. "I must go home." She was too happy to be tired as she walked. When she came to the top of the hill, she looked across to New Moon. How beautiful it was, in the twilight shelter of the old trees!

———

Father Cassidy was as good as his word. Lofty John did not cut down the grove, although he insisted that Emily must ask him not to do so, and that she and Ilse must come and visit him again. "The Murrays aren't the only proud ones," he told Emily. "I'm not called Lofty John for nothing. But you could have asked me yourself. You didn't have to go to Father Cassidy."

Chapter 12

*M*ore Letters to Father

DECEMBER 18.

Dearest Father,

Cousin Jimmy says there will be a snowstorm tonight. I am glad we will have snow for Christmas. The Murray dinner will be at New Moon this year. Last year it was at Uncle Oliver's, but Cousin Jimmy had flu, so I stayed home with him. This year I will be in the thick of it.

Do you notice that my spelling is better? I hate to stop writing to look up a word, so I write my letter first and then I look up the words I'm not sure of. Sometimes I think a word is all right when it isn't, so there are still some mistakes, but not so many.

We had tests in school this week. I did well in everything except arithmetic. Miss Brownell said something about the questions and I did not

hear her. I was making up a story. It is called
"Madge's Secret."

My pig died last week. It is a *great finanshul loss*
to me. Maybe I shouldn't have named it Lofty
John.

Ilse is getting on real well in school now. She
has won the silver metal for the best reciter in
Queen's County. They had the contest in Shrewsbury and Aunt Laura took Ilse because Dr. Burnley wouldn't and Ilse won it. I wish Dr. Burnley
would love Ilse. I'm so glad *you* loved me, Father.

Dec. 22.

We had our school concert today. Everybody
came except Dr. Burnley and Aunt Elizabeth. I
wore my old brown dress. I wanted to, because
Ilse did not have a good dress, and I did not want
her to feel bad. At first Aunt Elizabeth was not
going to let me, because the Murrays should always be well dressed, but then I told her about
Ilse and she said I could.

Rhoda made fun of Ilse and me, but then she
got stuck in her recitation. Nobody else knew her
poem except me. I wasn't going to help her, after
everything she has done. Then I thought how I
would feel being stuck in front of a big crowd of

people, and I whispered it to her. It's strange, Father, but now I don't hate Rhoda anymore.

DEC. 28.

Christmas is over. It was pretty nice. Uncle Wallace and Aunt Eva and Uncle Oliver and Aunt Addie and Aunt Ruth were here. Ilse and Dr. Burnley were here too.

I wore my blue cashmere dress, and my hair was tied with blue ribbons, and Aunt Laura let me wear Mother's blue silk sash with pink daisies on it that she had when she was a little girl at New Moon. Aunt Ruth sniffed and said, "I hope you are better than you used to be, Emily." Then she told my that my shoelace was untyed.

When we went into the sitting room for dinner I stepped on Aunt Eva's train and Aunt Ruth said, "What a clumsy child you are, Emily." I stuck my tongue out at her, but not so anyone could see. Cousin Jimmy carved the turkey and he gave me two slices of the breast. Aunt Ruth said, "When I was a child a wing was good enough for me," and Cousin Jimmy put another slice of breast on my plate. Aunt Ruth sniffed. Then she said, "I saw your teacher in town, Emily, and she did not say good things about you. If you were *my* daughter, I would not be at all pleased." "I am glad I am not your daughter," I said, but I did not say it out loud, just in my head. Aunt Ruth said, "Don't look so sulky when I talk to you, Emily," and Uncle Wallace said, "It's too bad she looks like that." "I see there is an ink stain on her finger," said Aunt Ruth. (I had been writing a poem before dinner.)

Then I got a surprise. Relations are always surprising you. Aunt Elizabeth said, *"I do wish, Ruth, that you and Wallace would leave that child alone."* I could hardly believe my ears.

After that the dinner was nice. They told stories and jokes about the Murrays. Aunt Elizabeth opened Grandfather Murray's desk and took out an old poem that had been written to Aunt Nancy *by a lover* when she was young. I said, "Was Great-aunt Nancy really as pretty as that?" and Uncle Wallace said, "They say she was, seventy years ago." I wonder if anybody will ever write a poem to me. If I could have bangs somebody might.

After dinner, we had presents. That is a Murray tradishun. My relations all gave me useful presents except Aunt Laura. She gave me a bottle of perfume.

Perry had Christmas with his aunt Tom. I gave

him and Teddy handkerchiefs, and I gave Ilse a hair ribbon. I bought them out of my egg money. I won't have any more egg money for a long time because my hen has stopped laying.

After dinner Ilse and I played in the kitchen and Cousin Jimmy helped us make taffy. Everybody stayed for supper. Afterwards Uncle Wallace said (this is another Murray tradishun), ''Let us think of those who have gone before.'' I liked the way he said it. It was one of the times that I felt glad to be—partly—one of the Murrays.

Aunt Laura and I stood out on the porch to see everybody leave. Aunt Laura said, ''Your mother and I used to stand here, Emily, to watch the Christmas guests go away.'' The snow creaked and the bells rang through the trees and the frost sparkled on the roof, and the flash came, Father, and that was best of all.

Chapter 13

*B*angs—and a Visit

Emily and Ilse were sliding on the frozen pond with Teddy Kent one day. Neither girl had skates, so Teddy was pulling them, one at a time. Ilse was waiting for her turn, her golden hair springing out around her face, her cheeks red from the wind. "Isn't Ilse lovely?" said Teddy.

Emily was not jealous, but she wanted to be lovely as well. If only Aunt Elizabeth would let her have bangs! That night when she undid her braids, Emily brushed her hair across her forehead and looked in the mirror. If she cut the bangs herself, Aunt Elizabeth would punish her, but she wouldn't be able to glue the hair back on! Emily got out the scissors and *snip, snip,* she made the cut. A fringe of hair curled softly above her eyebrows, hiding her high forehead.

It was exactly what she wanted. Emily looked at her reflection in triumph.

Then she started to think. Aunt Elizabeth would be furious, and she would have a right to be. The more she thought about it, the worse Emily felt. At last she took the scissors again and cut off the bangs as short as she could, but it was no use. Anyone could see that bangs had been cut, and now Emily looked a fright. She jumped into bed just as Aunt Elizabeth came in.

Aunt Elizabeth undressed and got into bed herself. The room was dark. Emily's feet were ice cold, but she did not think she ought to put them on the hot jar to warm them up. "Stop wriggling, Emily," said Aunt Elizabeth. Then "Ow!" She had put her own foot against Emily's. "Goodness, child, your feet are like snow. Here, put them on the jar." She pushed it against Emily's feet. How warm it was!

Emily felt worse than ever. "Aunt Elizabeth," she said, "I've got something to confess. I—I cut bangs."

"Bangs?" Aunt Elizabeth sat up in bed.

"But I cut them off again," said Emily in a hurry. "All of it, close to my head."

Aunt Elizabeth got out of bed and lit a candle. "You have made a sight of yourself," she said at last.

"I never saw anyone uglier than you are right now. And you have behaved very badly."

Emily had to agree. "I'm sorry," she said.

"You will eat supper alone for a week," said Aunt Elizabeth, "and I won't take you to Uncle Oliver's."

Emily's curls grew into the bangs she wanted, although she knew that as soon as her hair was long enough, Aunt Elizabeth would make her brush it back again. The bangs were at their best when Great-aunt Nancy asked for a photograph. "I'd like to see what Juliet's daughter looks like," she wrote. "Her father was a fascinating man."

"I'm glad this happened while I have my bangs," thought Emily happily.

But in the photographer's studio, Aunt Elizabeth brushed Emily's hair back and fastened it with hairpins. Emily looked hideous, all forehead, and sulky as well. When Aunt Elizabeth wrapped up the photograph and told Emily to take it to the post office, Emily decided to send Teddy's watercolor painting of her instead. She wrapped up her portrait in Aunt Elizabeth's cardboard and wrote a letter to go in the parcel:

Dear Great-aunt Nancy:
Aunt Elizabeth had my picture taken, but it is

ugly. An artist friend made this picture for me. It is just like me when I have bangs. I am just lending it to you, not giving it, because I valew it very much.

P.S. I am not so stupid as you think.

P.S. No. 2. I am not stupid *at all*.

Emily mailed her parcel and started home, feeling much better.

⌐

No reply came from Great-aunt Nancy. Aunt Laura and Aunt Elizabeth were not surprised, but Emily kept looking for a letter. At last she decided that Great-aunt Nancy was a rude old woman and wrote a letter telling her so. She hid the letter in the garret along with her letters to her father.

In July a letter came at last, inviting Emily to visit Great-aunt Nancy at Wyther Grange. Elizabeth and Laura talked it over in the cookhouse, forgetting that Emily was sitting on the steps outside.

"Should we let her go?" asked Elizabeth.

"Aunt Nancy seems to want her," said Laura.

"By the time she gets there, Nancy may have changed her mind."

"But if we don't, she'll never forgive us, or her. Emily should have her chance."

"It's not worth much. If Aunt Nancy has any money, she'll likely leave it to the Priests. And you know the way she talks, her and that awful old Caroline."

"Emily is too young to understand," said Aunt Laura.

"I understand lots," cried Emily, getting up.

Aunt Elizabeth jerked the door open. "Emily Starr, haven't you learned yet not to listen?"

"I wasn't listening," said Emily. "You knew I was sitting here. I can't help hearing. If you whisper, I know you're talking secrets, but you didn't whisper. Am I going to visit Great-aunt Nancy?"

"We haven't decided," said Aunt Elizabeth.

A week later Aunt Elizabeth brought a little black trunk down from the garret, and Emily knew she was to go.

"I wouldn't visit Wyther Grange for anything," said Ilse. "It's haunted."

"It's not."

"Is so, by things you can feel and hear, but never see. Your great-aunt Nancy is a crank, and the old woman who lives with her is a witch."

"She isn't."

"*Is*. She makes the stone dogs on the gateposts howl every night if anyone comes near the place. 'Wo-or-oo-oo.' " Ilse was the best reciter in Queen's County. She could have frightened Emily at night. But it was daytime.

"You're jealous," said Emily, and walked away.

"I'm not, you centipede," yelled Ilse. But next morning she came to say goodbye and ask Emily to write every week. Emily was going to drive to Priest Pond with Old Kelly. Her little black trunk was tied up on top of his red wagon, and they went clinking away down New Moon Lane.

"Get up, my nag, get up," said Old Kelly. "An' so ye're going to visit the old lady at Priest Pond. Ever been there?"

"No."

"It's full of Priests. They're as proud as the Murrays themselves. Look here, gurrl dear, don't ever marry a Priest."

"Why not?" Emily had never thought of marrying a Priest, but she had to know what he meant.

"They're bad to marry, hard to live with. The wives die young, all except the old lady at the Grange. The only decent one is Jarback Priest, and he's too old for you."

"Why do they call him Jarback?"

"One av his shoulders is higher than the other. A bookworm, I'm told. Have ye got a bit av iron?"

"No, why?"

"You should have. Old Caroline Priest at the Grange is a witch if there ever was one."

"That's what Ilse said. But, Mr. Kelly, there are no witches, you know that."

"Sure, sure." Old Kelly fished in his pocket. "Here, put this horseshoe nail in your pocket. It's better to be on the safe side."

The road to Priest Pond wound along the seashore, crossing rivers and edging the ponds. It was dusk when they reached Wyther Grange. The hall door was open, and they could see a little woman standing there. Old Kelly swung Emily and her box quickly to the ground. "Don't lose your bit av a nail," he whispered.

"So this is Emily of New Moon!" Emily heard a shrill voice saying. A hand like a claw reached out for hers. Emily knew there were no witches, but her other hand hung on to the nail as she went inside.

"Your aunt is in the back parlor," said Caroline Priest, leading the way. They went through a wide hall, with big, rich rooms on both sides, then through the kitchen into a narrow hall with four small windows on one side and high black cupboards on the other. Emily shivered. If Wyther Grange had been a castle, this would be the way to the dungeon. She followed Caroline up some stairs, through a room with a table set for supper, then down four more stairs into a bedroom. Here sat Great-aunt Nancy with her black cane leaning against her knee and her tiny white hands sparkling with rings.

Great-aunt Nancy, who had been so beautiful, was yellow-skinned and wrinkled, though her brown eyes were still bright. "So this is Juliet's girl," she said. "Now, Caroline, who does she look like?"

"Not as good-looking as the Murrays," said Caroline.

"Nor the Starrs either," said Great-aunt Nancy. "Her father was a handsome man. You are not as good-looking as your picture, Emily. Where are your bangs?"

"Aunt Elizabeth combed them back."

"Well, you comb them down again while you're in my house."

"Great-aunt Nancy," said Emily, "I'm glad I don't look like other people. I look like myself."

Aunt Nancy chuckled. "So you're not stupid, eh?"

"No, I'm not."

"Good. Brains are better than beauty. Brains last,

beauty doesn't. Look at me. Come, let's have supper.'' Aunt Nancy hobbled down the steps, using her cane.

''Why did you write such a stupid letter?'' Aunt Nancy asked as soon as they were sitting down.

''Because Aunt Elizabeth said she was going to read it.''

''Well, you can write what you like here, and say what you like, and do what you like. And you can pick a beau from the Priest boys.''

''I don't want a beau,'' said Emily.

''Don't tell me,'' laughed Aunt Nancy. ''When I was twelve I had half a dozen. All the little boys in Blair Water were fighting about me. Caroline, do you see what a pretty hand Emily has? As pretty as mine when I was young. Let's have a look at your ankles, puss.''

Emily, feeling uncomfortable, put out her foot. ''You've got Mary Shipley's ankle,'' said Aunt Nancy, ''a shapely ankle, just like mine. Almost all the Murray girls have thick ankles, yes, your mother too. You aren't beautiful, but men will think you are. Have another cookie, Emily.''

''I haven't had one yet,'' said Emily. She had been waiting for the cookies to be passed. Aunt Nancy and Caroline both laughed.

"What do you think of us?" asked Aunt Nancy.

Emily had been thinking that Aunt Nancy looked withered and shriveled, but she could not possibly say *that*!

"You think," said Aunt Nancy, "that I'm a hideous old hag and Caroline isn't quite human. Caroline, I wish you didn't have a wart on your nose."

"I wish you had one on your tongue," said Caroline.

Emily felt very tired. It was interesting, and Aunt Nancy was kind in her queer way, but she was homesick for New Moon. "The child's tired," said Aunt Nancy. "Put her in the pink bedroom, Caroline."

It was the first time Emily had ever slept in a room by herself. The pink bedroom was big and shadowy, with pink curtains and pink wallpaper with roses in a diamond pattern. The window was open. "Good night," said Caroline. "Nancy and I sleep in the old part of the house, and the rest of us sleep well in our graves." She went out and shut the door. Emily blew out the lamp. A dog began to howl. Emily was sure she could hear noises in the hall.

Then she did hear noises, right behind the wall at the head of her bed. There were strange rustling sounds, and low sounds like children's cries. They would stop for a little while and then begin again.

Emily hid under the covers, cold with terror. Ilse was right; Wyther Grange was haunted. It was cruel of Aunt Nancy to put her in a haunted room. Oh, if she were only back at dear New Moon, with Aunt Elizabeth in bed beside her.

All the rest of her life, Emily never forgot that night. She was so tired that sometimes she fell asleep for a few minutes; then the rustling and moaning woke her again. When morning came, the room was sunny and the sounds had stopped. Emily got dressed and went to look for Aunt Nancy.

"How did you sleep?" asked the old woman.

"I want to go home today," said Emily.

Aunt Nancy stared. "Nonsense," she said. "For one thing, there is no one to drive you."

"Then I will walk," said Emily.

Aunt Nancy glared at her. "Sit down and have your breakfast," she said.

"I won't," cried Emily. "I won't stay another night in that haunted room. It was cruel of you to put me there."

"What's this? We don't have ghosts at Wyther Grange, have we, Caroline?"

"They moaned and cried all night long in the wall behind my bed. I won't stay—I won't." Emily burst out crying.

Aunt Nancy and Caroline looked at each other.
"Poor child," said Aunt Nancy. "Caroline, it's your
fault, you should have reminded me. No wonder she
was frightened. We should have told her."

"Told me—what?"

"About the swallows in the chimney. That was
what you heard. That chimney isn't used for fires
anymore, and the swallows nest there, hundreds of
them. They do make an uncanny noise."

Emily felt foolish, though the same sounds had
frightened other people in times gone by. Aunt
Nancy and Caroline were both very kind to her all
day. She had a nap in the afternoon, and slept well
that night in the pink room. Swallows! They were
not scary at all.

Chapter 14

———

She Couldn't Have Done It

JULY 20.

Dear Father:

I thought I would never be happy at Wyther Grange, but I am, only it is different from New Moon happiness.

Aunt Nancy and Caroline let me do exactly what I like. They fight a lot, but I think they are like Ilse and me and love each other hard when they are not fighting. Aunt Nancy doesn't walk much because of her roomatism, so she reads and knits and plays cards with Caroline. I talk to her a lot, but I have never told her I write poetry. She would make me recite it, and she is not the right person to recite my poetry to.

She and Caroline talk about things that happened in the Priest and Murray families, and they never stop when they get to the interesting parts. Some things I don't understand, but I will someday. I am not to call Aunt Nancy Great-aunt. She says it makes her feel old. She tells me about all the men who were in love with her. It doesn't sound exciting, but she says it was.

There are many interesting things in the house. There is a Jakobite glass that belonged to an old ansester of the Priests long ago in Scotland. It is a very valewable airloom. And there is a pickled snake in a big glass jar. I look at it every day. Something seems to drag me to it. The thing I like best is a big shining ball that hangs from the lamp in the living room. Aunt Nancy says I am to have it when she is dead. It is a Murray airloom.

Sunday is fun here, but not holy. Nice for a change. Aunt Nancy can't go to church, so she and Caroline play cards all day. In the afternoon some of the Priests come to visit and stay for supper. When they go away again, Aunt Nancy makes fun of them to Caroline, and Caroline gets angry because she is a Priest, so they always fight on Sunday nights.

The place I like best is down by the bay shore. Some parts are very steep. I wander there and compose poetry.

Aunt Nancy doesn't like Aunt Elizabeth. She

said, "Elizabeth Murray killed Jimmy's mind because of her temper. If she had killed his body, she would have been a murderess. I think killing his mind was worse."

I do not like Aunt Elizabeth at times myself, but I felt I had to stand up for her. I gave Aunt Nancy a *look* and said, "Don't say things like that about my aunt Elizabeth."

Aunt Nancy said, "Well, Saucebox, if you don't like what I'm saying, don't hang around. I notice there are plenty of things you like to hear."

July 22.

Oh, dear Father, I have broken Aunt Nancy's Jakobite glass. It seems like a dreadful dream. I went to look at the pickled snake and my sleeve caught the Jakobite glass and it smashed into a thousand pieces. I hid them in a box behind the sofa. Maybe they won't miss the glass until I am gone. I know Aunt Nancy will never forgive me when she finds out. I can't stop thinking about it.

July 24.

Dear Father, this is a very strange world. Nothing turns out like what you expect. Last night I couldn't sleep again. At last I went to find Aunt

Nancy. She was all alone, playing cards. I just said,
"I broke your Jakobite glass yesterday and hid the
pieces behind the sofa." Aunt Nancy said "What a
blessing. All the Priest clan are waiting for me to
die so that they can fight over it, and now they
can't. Get off to bed and get your beauty sleep." I
said, "Aren't you mad at me?" and she said, "If it
had been a Murray airloom I would be, but I don't
care a rap about the Priest things."

JULY 28.

Oh, Father dear, I have found out all about the
mistery of Ilse's mother. It is so terrible I can't
write it down, even to you. I did not think there
could be such terrible things in the world. No, I
can't believe it, and I won't believe it. I *know* Ilse's
mother couldn't have done that.

Great-aunt Nancy and Caroline loved to tell each
other old family stories. They liked all the details,
the wicked stories more than the happy ones. And so
one afternoon they started on the story of Allan
Burnley's marriage.

Aunt Nancy put down her cards. "Emily," she
said, "do you think your aunt Laura is going to
marry Dr. Burnley?"

"Of course not," said Emily. "Dr. Burnley hates women."

"It's eleven years now since his wife ran away; he might have got over it."

"I never heard all that story," said Caroline. "Who was his wife?"

"Beatrice Mitchell. She was only eighteen when Allan married her, and he was thirty-five."

"Was she beautiful?"

Aunt Nancy sniffed. "Pretty, I'd say, with golden hair all round her face. She had a birthmark on her forehead, just like a tiny red heart. She certainly seemed to be in love with Allan, but that's too much of a difference in their ages; you might have known there would be trouble. Her cousin Leo was at sea when she got married. Folks said he'd been in love with her, and when he got home he came to see her all the time. Allan Burnley never thought anything of it, but then Leo's ship was due to sail and she went to see him off and ran away with him."

"Did she, then?" said Caroline. "What happened?"

"The ship went down in a storm and everybody drowned, and that was the end of that elopement, and of Beatrice with her golden hair and her ace of hearts."

"No," cried Emily. She stood up, holding out her hands as if she could push the dreadful story away. "Ilse's mother didn't do *that*! She didn't run away and leave her little baby, not Ilse's mother."

"Catch her, Caroline," said Aunt Nancy. She thought Emily was going to faint.

"Don't touch me," cried Emily. "You—you *liked* hearing that horrible story!"

She rushed out of the room. Aunt Nancy shook her head. "I thought she would have heard all about it long ago," she said.

Emily cried for hours. Ilse's mother had run away and left her little baby. No, there must be some mistake, Ilse's mother couldn't have done *that*!

Ilse didn't know the story, and Emily hated to think of going back to New Moon with such an awful secret. She could not stop thinking about it, day and night. Aunt Nancy and old Caroline didn't tell any more hateful stories when Emily could hear them, but they didn't seem to want her company now that they had to be careful what they said. Most days Emily walked on the bay shore, wondering how she could prove Ilse's mother had not run away. It seemed as if that dark mystery would never be solved.

Chapter 15

—

Freedom Lost, and Freedom Won

Emily wandered one evening farther than she had ever gone before. She was just going to turn back when she saw a wild aster on the edge of the bank. She had never seen such a big one before, and at once she knew she must have it.

As she bent to pick it, the ground moved under her, and the bank gave way. Emily found herself slipping and sliding down toward the rocks, thirty feet below. Then she stopped. The clump of earth that had fallen with her was caught on a narrow ledge, and Emily lay there, hardly daring to breathe. If she moved at all, she would fall to her death.

Suddenly she saw a man's face peering over the bank. One shoulder was higher than the other, and Emily knew this must be Mr. Dean

Priest, nicknamed Jarback. He seemed as frightened as she was. "What can I do?" he said. "I can't help you; I'll have to go for a rope, and I can't go fast. I'm a bit lame. Can you hold on?"

Emily breathed a "Yes."

"I'll leave my dog with you," said the man. "Here, Tweed, just look at her. Don't even wag your tail."

Now Emily had the drama of her rescue to think about. The big dog sat still. Emily had never had a dog, but Tweed was very comforting. "I love cats to live with," she thought, "but perhaps dogs are better in an emergency."

Dean Priest came back sooner than she had expected. "I found some rope in a boat down the shore," he said. "I'm going to drop it to you. Can you hold on while I pull you up?"

"I'll try," whispered Emily.

He wrapped the rope around a tree, then made a loop in the other end and threw it down. Emily caught it. At once the rope took the weight of her whole body as the clump of earth fell to the cruel rocks below. Emily got a knee on the ledge and hung on, scrabbling with her toes as Dean Priest pulled her up. As she went by, she reached out and picked the big aster. "I've got you!" she exclaimed. Then she remembered her manners. ''Thank you very much,'' she said. ''I think I'll sit down now.'' Now that she was safe, she was trembling.

Her rescuer sat down also, with his back against a tree. He seemed to be trembling himself. ''Do you know who I am?'' he asked.

''I think you must be Jar— Mr. Dean Priest, I mean,'' said Emily.

''Jarback.'' He laughed, not a nice laugh. ''That's what they call me. But who are you? What are you doing here?''

Emily explained.

''I knew your father,'' he told her. ''We were good friends at school.'' Dean Priest never forgot Emily's face as he had seen it when he looked over the bank, the still white face and the big dark eyes. ''I think I'll wait for you,'' he said.

''I'm ready to go now,'' said Emily.

''That wasn't what I meant,'' he laughed. They got up and started back, with the big dog walking between them. Emily found herself telling Dean Priest about her poetry and reciting her best pieces.

''Let's see,'' he said, ''you're twelve now.''

''And three months,'' said Emily.

''In ten years, you may do something.''

"Father Cassidy told me to keep on," said Emily happily.

"Oh, you'll keep on; nobody could stop you."

"I'm going to be a famous poetess or a great novelist," said Emily.

Dean Priest smiled. "Better be a novelist," he told her, "I hear it pays better."

"I've only got one problem," admitted Emily. "I can't write love talk. I can do everything else."

"I'll teach you," he said, "when you're older."

"Thank you," said Emily. "And thank you again for saving me."

"Oh," he said, partly teasing, "now that I've saved you, your life belongs to me. You paid a high price for your flower, Emily."

Emily threw down the big aster and tramped on it. But when she had gone into the house, Dean Priest picked it up and took it home and pressed it between the pages of a book.

Emily spent the next few days with her new friend and his dog, but then suddenly Aunt Nancy said, "I like you, Emily, but I'm tired of you; it's time you went home." Emily's feelings were hurt, but when she thought about it, she really wanted to go back to New Moon.

Cousin Jimmy drove over to get her. They had so much to talk about that the drive seemed very short. Aunt Laura came running out to meet them. Aunt Elizabeth had made cream puffs, Emily's favorite, for supper. Perry was waiting to tell her about kittens and calves and pigs and the new foal. Ilse came over, and she and Emily got into a fight over Saucy Sal's new kitten. "Emily, if you and Ilse fight over this kitten, it'll have to go," said Aunt Elizabeth.

Emily made peace with Ilse by letting her name the kitten, and Ilse named it Daffodil. "I'll call it Daff," Emily decided.

After supper, Emily heard Teddy's special whistle and ran out to meet him. They scampered happily up to the Tansy Patch to see a new puppy that Dr. Burnley had given to Teddy. "I've always wanted a dog, but I don't think Mother will let me keep him," said Teddy gloomily. "If anything happens to him, I know it will be her fault."

"Tell her that," said Emily. "Tell her if anything happens to your puppy, you'll believe it is her fault. She'll take good care of him, you'll see." Emily sounded just like Aunt Elizabeth when she said, "It is the best thing to do."

"I will," said Teddy. "That's very clever of you. Oh, Emily, I'm glad you're back."

Emily went home happily. The candles were lighted in the New Moon kitchen. "I suppose you like lamps better now," said Aunt Laura.

Emily looked at the candles. "I don't know, Aunt Laura," she said. "You can be friends with candles. I think I like candles best."

Aunt Elizabeth smiled. "You have some sense in you," she said.

"That's the second compliment you've paid me," thought Emily. "Perhaps you do like me a little, Aunt Elizabeth."

"You're old enough now for a room of your own," said Aunt Elizabeth. "Laura and I have decided that you are to have your mother's room."

Emily was thrilled. Her mother's room had always been locked, and she had never seen it. Aunt Laura took her up. Emily set down her candle and looked around her. "My very own room," she said, loving it from the first glance. It was old-fashioned, like all the New Moon rooms. The wallpaper had a design of golden diamond shapes and golden stars, and the walls were hung with embroidered samplers and mottoes and old-fashioned pictures cut from magazines. There were braided rugs on the floor. The bed was high, with carved black posts but, Emily was glad to see, no curtains. There was a little washstand with a blue basin and jug, two high-backed chairs, and even a little fireplace.

A picture of her mother when she was a little girl hung over the mantel. Emily suddenly found herself feeling very close to her. "Oh, Mother," she said, "what did you think about when you lived here? I wish I had known you then." When she wrote to her father a few days later, she began the letter, "Dear Father and Mother."

I'm sorry I left you out so long, but you didn't seem real until that night I came home. I like to go to bed early now.

Oh Father dear and Mother, we are going to have a new teacher. Miss Brownell is going to be married. Ilse says her father said, "God help the man." Our new teacher is a Mr. Carpenter. He is married, and he is going to live in the little old house below the school.

Aunt Elizabeth looked cross when she saw my bangs, but she didn't say anything. Aunt Laura said to just go on wearing them, but I don't like to go against Aunt Elizabeth, so I combed them all back except just a little bit.

Teddy and I went up to the Disappointed House yesterday, and we found a loose board and we got inside. It is not plastered, and the shavings are lying all over the floor the way the carpenters left them all those years ago. I felt like crying. We made a tiny fire in the fireplace and sat down and talked. We decided when we grow up we will buy the Disappointed House and live there together and Teddy will paint and I will write and we will have toast and marmalade and bacon every morning for breakfast. Teddy said we'd have to get married, but I thought maybe we wouldn't need to bother. When the fire burned out, we jammed the board back and came away.

Ilse and I have only had two fights since I came home. She called me a sneaking albatross today. I wonder how many animals are left. She never says the same one twice. I felt very queer when I saw Ilse at first, because I know about her mother. Sometimes I feel very unhappy about it. I wish I could forget about it, or find out what really happened, but I can't.

> Your lovingest daughter,
> Emily

Chapter 16

A Weaver of Dreams

Emily wasn't sure at first if she liked Mr. Carpenter or not, nor were the others, except Ilse, who liked him from the start. He was a tall man, between forty and fifty years old, with bushy gray hair and a mustache, bright blue eyes, and a long, grayish face.

He had a bad temper and usually blew up at least once a day, but he was never mean, so the children did not mind. One day he yelled at Perry, "Do you hear me? Do you?"

"Of course I hear you," said Perry coolly. "They could hear you in Charlottetown."

Mr. Carpenter stared at him, then broke into a jolly laugh.

He turned everything they were used to upside down. Miss Brownell had insisted on order. Mr. Carpenter did not, but he kept the children so busy they had no time for mischief. When he taught history, they played the different characters and acted out everything. If you were Mary, Queen of Scots, beheaded by Perry Miller wearing a mask made out of Aunt Laura's old black silk dress, you did not forget the year it happened. If you fought the battle of Waterloo with Teddy Kent leading the charge, you remembered 1815.

On Friday afternoons Mr. Carpenter made everybody recite poems and make speeches. This was the day Ilse loved, even if Mr. Carpenter was hard on her.

One day Mr. Carpenter picked up Teddy's slate and found a picture of himself. It did not flatter him, but he chuckled over it and told Teddy not to bother doing extra arithmetic in the afternoons. ''You'd better draw pictures,'' he said.

Mr. Carpenter went up to the Tansy Patch that evening and saw Teddy's sketches in the old barn loft. Then he went into the house and talked to Mrs. Kent. He went away looking grim, and afterward he gave Teddy some books on art and told him not to take them home. Teddy knew that they would disappear if he did. He wished his mother was more like other people's mothers, but they did love each other very much.

Mr. Carpenter was hard on Perry over his speeches, and he was hard on Emily over her compositions. Emily sometimes took out her old poems to read, and was surprised to find they were not nearly as good as they had seemed to her when she wrote them. One day she took a lot of them downstairs and burned them in the stove.

Emily shot up that winter. Aunt Laura had to let down her dresses. Uncle Wallace looked at her one day when he was visiting. "How old are you, Emily?" he asked.

"Thirteen in May."

"Hm. She should be trained to make her living," he told Aunt Elizabeth.

"The Murray women have never had to work out," said Aunt Elizabeth.

"Emily is only half Murray," said Uncle Wallace. "You and Laura won't live forever, Elizabeth, and when you die New Moon goes to Oliver's Andrew. Emily should be sent to Queen's to get her teacher's license. I will help with the expense. I'm sure Emily would rather earn her living than live on charity."

"I would, I would," cried Emily. "Please, Aunt Elizabeth, I'll pay back every cent it costs."

"It is not a matter of money," said Aunt Elizabeth. "I am not against education, Emily. I may send you to high school in Shrewsbury for a couple of years, but you are not going to be a slave to the public—no Murray girl ever was *that*!''

Emily decided she would have to make her living by writing, so she wrote more poetry than ever. She thought about starting a novel, but she did not have enough paper, even though a new Jimmy-book always appeared, as if by magic, when the old one was nearly full.

Chapter 17

—

Sacrilege

Aunt Elizabeth and Emily had various battles that winter and spring, but the worst ones were over Emily's writing. Aunt Elizabeth had thought she was writing compositions for school. Stories were different! Aunt Elizabeth really believed it was wrong to write anything that was not true. "Don't you know it is wicked to write novels?" she asked.

"I'm not writing novels yet," said Emily. "I don't have enough paper. But it isn't wicked, Aunt Elizabeth—Father liked novels."

"Your father—" began Aunt Elizabeth, and stopped. She knew Emily would not put up with any criticism of her father, but she was angry because she could not say what she wanted. "You will not write any more of this stuff," she commanded. "I forbid you."

"I can't stop writing stories, Aunt Elizabeth," Emily tried to explain. "It's *in* me. Teddy has to paint, and Ilse has to recite, and I have to write stories. Don't you *see,* Aunt Elizabeth?"

"I see you are an ungrateful, disobedient child," said Aunt Elizabeth.

This hurt Emily badly, especially as Aunt Laura did not understand either. "I do think you could stop writing," she said, "to please your aunt. I know you like to do it, and I don't see any harm in it myself, but it's not anything that matters much, and it is a waste of time."

"No, no," said Emily. "Someday I'll write real books, Aunt Laura, and make a lot of money," she added, thinking Aunt Laura would like that idea.

Aunt Laura just smiled. "You'll never make money that way," she said. "You'd better learn something useful. Emily, if you really can't stop writing, try not to let Elizabeth see you at it."

But Emily could not pretend she was not writing, even though she hated to have Aunt Elizabeth think badly of her. She wrote a very long letter to her father about it.

There was a huge bundle of letters by now on the shelf in the garret, and one day while Emily was at the Tansy Patch, Aunt Elizabeth, housecleaning, found and read them all. Elizabeth Murray would never have read somebody else's letters if the somebody else had been a grown-up, but she felt she had a right to know everything about Emily.

The letters were a shock. Emily had often been furious with Aunt Elizabeth when she wrote them, and her words were merciless. Nobody had ever dared to say such things to Elizabeth Murray. As she folded the last letter, her hands trembled.

When Emily came home, Aunt Elizabeth was waiting for her in the parlor. Emily couldn't remember doing anything bad, but as soon as she opened the door and saw her aunt with the bundle of letters on her lap, she understood. She flew across the room and snatched them.

"How dare you?" she said. "How dare you touch *my private papers,* Aunt Elizabeth?"

Aunt Elizabeth had not expected *this.* Emily seemed to think *she* was the guilty one! "Give me those letters," she said.

"I will not," said Emily, white with rage. "You had no right to touch them. I will *never* forgive you."

Aunt Elizabeth sat with her mouth open for a moment. She had expected shame, perhaps, or fear, certainly not rage. For the first time in her life, Elizabeth Murray wondered if she had done something wrong. They faced each other, the tall old woman white-faced and thin-lipped, the child trembling, hugging her letters. "I took you in. I have given you food and shelter and education and kindness," said Elizabeth at last, "and this is how you thank me!"

"You did not *want* to take me," said Emily. "None of you wanted me, only you were the proud Murrays, so one of you had to. You made me draw lots, that's why I'm here. Aunt Laura loves me now, but you don't, so why should I love you?"

"Thankless child."

"I'm not! I've tried to be good. I do all the chores I can to help pay for my keep. And you had *no business* to read my letters."

"They must be burned!"

"No. I'd rather burn myself." Emily felt the Murray look on her face, and knew she was winning.

"Keep your letters then," said Aunt Elizabeth bitterly, "and scorn the old woman who opened her home to you." She left the room.

Emily had won this battle, but victory brought no joy. She went and hid her letters in her own room, then lay down on her bed. Aunt Elizabeth was not just angry, she was hurt as well. Emily, thinking of her letters, knew she had not always been fair to Aunt Elizabeth, and certainly she had not been kind.

Emily's own eyes stung as she thought about the hurt in Aunt Elizabeth's. It was true that Aunt Elizabeth had not wanted her, but she had taken her. It was hardly honorable to have written about Aunt Elizabeth's faults while she was living under Aunt Elizabeth's roof. "I must find her and say I'm sorry," Emily decided at last.

She was just starting to get up when Aunt Elizabeth came in. Then something amazing happened. "Emily, I admit I had no right to read your letters," Aunt Elizabeth said stiffly. "Will you forgive me?"

Emily flung her arms around Aunt Elizabeth. "Oh," she gulped, "I'm sorry—I'm sorry—I didn't mean *all* those things I wrote, truly, I didn't mean the worst of them."

"I'd like to believe that, Emily. I don't like to think you hate me, my sister's child, little Juliet's child."

"I don't, I don't," sobbed Emily. "And I'll love you, Aunt Elizabeth, if you want me to. *Dear*

Aunt Elizabeth.'' Emily gave Aunt Elizabeth a
fierce hug.

Aunt Elizabeth kissed her forehead. ''You'd better
wash your face,'' she said, ''and come to supper.''

Emily put the letters away. She knew Aunt Elizabeth would not read her private papers again.

Chapter 18

⌒

*W*hen the Curtain Lifted

Emily's life that summer was rich and full. She and Aunt Elizabeth would never see everything the same way. But Aunt Elizabeth had learned that there is not one law of fairness for children and a different one for grown-ups. And Emily had learned that Aunt Elizabeth really cared for her. It made a huge difference. "I don't believe I'm a duty to Aunt Elizabeth anymore," she thought happily.

"I've no patience with Allan Burnley," said Aunt Elizabeth to Laura one afternoon. "He orders me to do this or that for Emily, but he neglects his own child, just because her mother wasn't all she was supposed to be—as if the child was to blame for that!"

"Shhh," said Aunt Laura, seeing Emily.

"No point in 'shhhing,'" thought Emily. "I

know the story about Ilse's mother. I just don't believe it.'' She went slowly upstairs. She was writing a
story called *The Ghost of the Well,* about Silas and
Thomas Lee and the old well in the field, but when
she sat down with pen and paper, no words came.
She felt very tired, and her head ached. She lay down
and found that she was worrying about Ilse's mother
again, and worrying about how her story was going
to end. Her eyes hurt, and she was cold, although it
was a hot July day.

She was still lying down when Aunt Elizabeth
came to see why she had not gone to get the cows.
''I didn't know it was so late,'' said Emily. ''Aunt
Elizabeth, my head aches.''

Aunt Elizabeth rolled up the blind and looked at
Emily; then she sent Perry for the doctor. ''Measles,
I expect,'' said Dr. Burnley. ''There's a bad kind
going round. Some kids have died of it, but mostly
because they were out of bed when they shouldn't be
and caught cold. I don't think you need to worry
about Emily. Keep her warm and keep the room
dark.''

Aunt Elizabeth moved a couch into Emily's room
and slept there. Emily got sicker and sicker. On the
fifth day her fever shot up and she began to talk
wildly. Dr. Burnley was worried. ''I have to go to

the city," he said, "but I'll see you tomorrow night. What's this nonsense about the Wind Woman?"

"It's just her talk," said Aunt Elizabeth. "Allan, is there any danger?"

"There's always danger with this kind of measles," said the doctor. "She is worrying about something, isn't she? Emily, what is bothering you?"

Emily looked up with fever-bright eyes. "She *couldn't* have done it."

"Of course not," said the doctor. "Of course she didn't."

"What are you talking about—dear?" asked Aunt Elizabeth. It was the first time she had called Emily "dear."

But Emily did not hear her. "Mr. Lee's well is open," she screamed. "Someone will fall into it and be killed. Why doesn't he shut it up?"

"I have to go," said Dr. Burnley. "Try to keep her quiet. Humor her, do whatever she wants, as much as you can. She shouldn't be fretting when she's so sick."

Aunt Elizabeth sat up with Emily until two o'clock; then Laura came. "She keeps saying, 'She *couldn't* have done it,' " said Aunt Elizabeth. "Oh, Laura, you remember the time I read her letters? Do you think she means me?"

Laura shook her head. She had never seen her sister so worried and sad. Elizabeth went quickly out of the room. Laura sat down by the bed. She loved Emily like her own child. Emily fell asleep but tossed and turned until dawn. Then she opened her eyes.

"I see her coming over the fields," she said in a high, clear voice. "She is singing, thinking of her baby. Oh, keep her back. She doesn't see the well— it's so dark she doesn't see it. Oh, she's gone into it!" Emily's voice rose to a scream.

Elizabeth came running. Laura was struggling with Emily. Her cheeks were bright red, and her eyes still had that faraway, wild look. "Emily, darling, you've had a bad dream. The old Lee well isn't open— nobody has fallen into it."

"Yes, she has," cried Emily. "I saw her, with the ace of hearts on her forehead."

Elizabeth and Laura stared at each other. "Who did you see, Emily?" asked Aunt Elizabeth.

"Ilse's mother, of course," said Emily. "I knew she didn't run away and leave her baby. She fell into the old well. Go and get her out, Aunt Laura."

"Yes, of course we will, darling," soothed Aunt Laura.

Emily sat up in bed and looked at her. "You are lying to me," she cried. "You are just saying that to put me off. Aunt Elizabeth''—she turned and caught Aunt Elizabeth's hand—''you'll do it for me, won't you?''

Aunt Elizabeth looked at Emily. ''Do whatever she wants, as much as you can,'' Dr. Burnley had told them. ''Yes, I'll get her out if she is in there,'' she said.

Emily let go of her hand and sank back into bed. The wild look left her eyes. ''I know you'll keep your word,'' she said. ''You are hard, but *you* never lie, Aunt Elizabeth.''

Elizabeth was still trembling when Laura came down and heard her giving orders to Cousin Jimmy in the kitchen. ''Elizabeth, you aren't really going to search the old well, are you?'' she asked. ''We'll be laughed at for a pair of fools!''

''I know it's nonsense,'' said Elizabeth, ''and I know we'll be laughed at, but I promised her, Laura. She trusted me, and I am going to keep my promise.''

—

Allan Burnley was gray with tiredness when he stepped into the New Moon kitchen at sunset. Cousin Jimmy looked at him strangely. ''Where are

Laura and Elizabeth?'' asked the doctor. ''How is Emily?''

''Emily is better,'' said Jimmy. ''Her rash has come out, and her fever is down. Laura and Elizabeth are in the sitting room.'' He added, in an eerie voice, ''There is nothing hidden that shall not be revealed.''

Why was Jimmy acting so oddly? Why weren't Elizabeth and Laura in the kitchen? Allan Burnley pushed open the sitting room door. Laura Murray sat on the couch, crying. Elizabeth, her back very straight, looked at him. She wore her second-best black silk dress, and she had been crying too.

Allan had never seen Elizabeth Murray cry. Something dreadful must have happened, something to do with him. An accident—or worse—to Ilse? In that ghastly moment, he knew he loved his child.

''Oh, Allan,'' said Elizabeth, ''God forgive us all.''

''It is—Ilse,'' said Dr. Burnley dully.

''No, not Ilse.'' And then she told him what they had found at the bottom of the old Lee well, what had really happened to his lovely young wife twelve long years before.

Emily did not see the doctor until the next evening. She was in bed, weak and limp, red with measles, but quite herself again. "Dear Emily," he said, "do you know what you have done for me? God knows how you did it."

"I thought you didn't believe in God," said Emily.

"You have given me back my faith," said Dr. Burnley.

"Why, what have I done?"

Dr. Burnley saw that Emily did not remember. "We'll tell you when you are better," he said.

"How could she know?" whispered Laura, in the kitchen.

"I don't know," said the doctor. "But she has given my dear wife back to me. I can remember Beatrice now with love. Oh, we might find ways to explain it. Emily has heard about Beatrice, that she ran off and left us, and she has worried about it. And the stories of the old Lee well made a deep impression on her—and then there was Jimmy's tumble into the New Moon well. We could say she mixed it all up when she was so sick she didn't know what she was saying. I might have explained it that way myself, once. Now, Laura, I don't know, I only know how thankful I am."

"They said our stepmother's mother had the sec-

ond sight,'' said Elizabeth. ''I never believed it—
before.''

The excitement had died down before Emily heard
the whole story. Ilse's mother had been buried, and
a stone in memory of the ''beloved wife of Allan
Burnley'' had been erected on her grave.

''I *knew* Ilse's mother couldn't have done it,'' said
Emily happily.

''We should have known it too,'' said Aunt Laura,
''but it did seem black against her at the time. Mr.
James Lee remembers the well was open that night.
His hired man was making a new cover when the
Greerson barn caught fire and they all ran to help.
By the time the fire was out, it was dark. Mr. Lee
fixed the new cover himself the next day. He didn't
look in the well, but he wouldn't have seen anything
if he had; the ferns would have hidden it. He never
thought Beatrice might have fallen in. You see, we all
knew she had gone on board her cousin's ship, and
nobody thought she came off again. But she did, and
you showed us the truth. But Emily, how could you
know?''

''I don't know. I didn't remember anything at
first, but now—it seems like a dream, seeing Ilse's
mother coming over the fields, singing. It was dark,

but I could see the ace of hearts——oh, Aunty, I don't like to think of it."

"We won't talk about it again," said Aunt Laura.

"And Ilse, does her father love her now?" asked Emily.

"He can't love her enough! He's making up for twelve years all at once," laughed Aunt Laura. "And she is just drinking it in. You'll see her soon, Emily, when we're sure there's no danger of infection."

"I didn't know anyone could be as happy as I am now," said Emily.

Chapter 19

&mily's Great Moment

One afternoon in October, Mr. Carpenter asked Emily to let him see some of her poems. "Probably you can't write decent poetry and never will," he said, "but let me see your work. If it's hopelessly bad, I'll tell you so. Then if you go on wasting your time, it won't be my fault. Bring some of your stories too."

Emily spent all evening choosing the poems. She added a Jimmy-book with her best new stories. The next day, the minutes crawled while she waited for school to end and everybody else to leave. Her whole future lay in Mr. Carpenter's hands. He picked up her work and sat in the seat in front of her, facing her. Emily was white and tense. Mr. Carpenter settled his glasses and began to read. Emily braced her feet against the legs of her desk to keep her knees from trembling.

"Humph!" said Mr. Carpenter. " *'Sunset'*—Lord, how many poems have been written on 'Sunset'? And this— *'To Life'*—'Life, as thy gift I ask no rainbow joy'—Is that true? Stop and think. Do you ask 'no rainbow joy' of life?"

"No," said Emily honestly. "I *do* want rainbow joy, lots of it."

"Of course you do. We all do, even if we don't get it. Don't say you don't, even in a poem. 'I weary of the hungry world'—what do you know of the hungry world?—but it *is* hungry. *'To Winter'*—must you write a poem for every season?—ha! 'Spring will not forget'—that's a good line, the only good line in it."

His voice went on. Emily writhed. Her poetry was no good. Why had she ever thought it was? Why had she shown it to him?

" 'When the morning light is shaken like a banner on the hill'—a good line, a good line—how old are you?"

"Thirteen, last May."

"Humph. *'Lines to Mrs. George Irving's Infant Son'*— your titles are as out of date as the candles at New Moon.

'Your azure dimples are the graves
Where million buried sunbeams play'——

Atrocious! Graves aren't playgrounds. How much would *you* play if you were buried?''

Emily blushed. Why couldn't she have seen that for herself? Any fool could have seen it.

Mr. Carpenter finished at last. Emily looked at him, waiting.

"Ten good lines out of four hundred, Emily—all the rest is balderdash.''

Emily's eyes filled with tears. She felt exactly like a candle that somebody had blown out.

"What are you crying for?'' demanded Mr. Carpenter.

"I'm sorry—you think it's no good.''

"No good! Didn't I tell you there were ten good lines? If you can write ten good lines when you're thirteen, at twenty you'll write ten times ten—if the gods are kind. You've got to work hard, Emily—by gad, girl, you've chosen a jealous goddess. She'll never let you go.''

He picked up the Jimmy-book. Emily shone with joy. "Emily B. Starr, the famous poet.'' "E. Byrd Starr, the great novelist.'' Which one would she be?

Mr. Carpenter chuckled. Emily stared at him.

There were only four of her stories in that book, and none of them was funny. "So you think I am not beautiful when I say my prayers?" said Mr. Carpenter.

Emily gasped. She had given him the wrong book! This one was full of wicked little word paintings of everybody in Blair Water, including him! Emily did not know how clever it was, but Mr. Carpenter did. He saw himself alive on Emily's page. She had drawn his bad side mercilessly, but his good side just as well.

"I'm sorry," said Emily, red with shame.

"Don't be! I wouldn't have missed this for all the poetry you'll ever write. Emily, why do you want to write?"

"I want to be famous and rich."

"Everybody does. Is that all?"

"No. I just *love* to write."

"That's better. Tell me, if you knew you would never make any money, never have a line published, would you go on writing?"

"Of course I would," said Emily. "Why, I *have* to write."

"Then you'll go on, no matter what I say. Thirteen years from now I may be famous because I was your teacher. Now, take your book and go home."

Emily went, her happiness lighting the world with golden glory. At sunset she sat in her room, watching Daffy chase dead leaves along the walks. Ilse and Perry and Teddy were waiting for her in Lofty John's grove, and soon she would go to them, but not yet. This was her private moment of joy. Once she would have written a letter to her father, but not now. On the table in front of her was a brand-new Jimmybook. She took her pen and wrote, on the first page,

New Moon, P.E. Island,
October 8th.

I am going to write a diary, to be published when I die.

About the Authors

Lucy Maud Montgomery was born on November 30, 1874, on Prince Edward Island, Canada. Her childhood on the island later inspired her most popular and beloved novel, *Anne of Green Gables,* which was published in 1908. In 1911 she married Reverend Ewan MacDonald; they settled in Toronto and had two sons. By the time of her death in 1942, L. M. Montgomery had written more than twenty books, including seven more books about Anne, and the Emily of New Moon trilogy.

Priscilla Galloway was born in Montreal and now lives in Toronto. She has taught at the high-school and university levels and has been honored as Teacher of the Year by the Ontario Council of Teachers of English. Her most recent book for Delacorte Press was *Truly Grim Tales,* an ALA Best Book for Young Adults and an ALA Quick Pick for Young

Adults. She has also published illustrated novels based on Greek mythology, as well as picture books and adult nonfiction. Her poetry and short stories have appeared in magazines and scholarly journals and have been broadcast by the Canadian Broadcasting Corporation.